SWEET TYRANNY

SWEET TYRANNY

Unemployed and homeless, Ann Ashley applied for a resident job looking after a small girl in the West Country. She got the job and thankfully left London behind to settle into the big house on the moors, but so much was unexplained. Why was this girl, who should have been at boarding school, to be kept away from other children? Why was handsome, arrogant Howard Crayne so edgy about the child even going out? And why was there a requirement in the advertisement – which she had ignored – that the applicant must have been jilted?

Sweet Tyranny

by

Jill Murray

Dales Large Print Books
Long Preston, North Yorkshire,
BD23 4ND, England.

British Library Cataloguing in Publication Data.

Murray, Jill
 Sweet tyranny.

 A catalogue record of this book is
 available from the British Library

 ISBN   978-1-84262-839-3 pbk

First published in Great Britain 1977 by Robert Hale Limited

Copyright © Jill Murray 1977

Cover illustration © Margie Hurwich by arrangement with
Arcangel Images

The moral right of the author has been asserted.

Published in Large Print 2011 by arrangement with
The Executor of Jill Murray
care of S. Walker Literary Agency

Dales Large Print is an imprint of Library Magna Books Ltd.

Printed and bound in Great Britain by
T.J. (International) Ltd., Cornwall, PL28 8RW

Love is a sweet tyranny, because the lover endureth his torments willingly.

Old proverb

ONE

Ann Ashley stared out of the train window and shivered a little at what she had done. Well, it was settled now, wasn't it? And it hadn't been entirely her doing. It seemed as if Fate had hustled her into it.

She wasn't looking at the scenery as it rushed by; scenery that changed from county to county, from the gentle landscape of Dorset and Somerset, through the lush greenness and the red earth of Devon, with now a hint of the harsh moorland of Cornwall appearing in view. As the journey lengthened, so her apprehensions intensified, but it was no use. She had burned her boats. Two new people were coming to the flat tomorrow, and she didn't know where Felicity would be.

Her hands gripped each other as she thought of that day when she had been filling their little flatlet with the good smells of baking. Felicity usually skidded to a halt on the doorstep and dramatised the moment, perhaps from an attack of conscience because she never took her turn at the shabby little stove, not even to make a cup of tea or boil an egg. That day, however, she had hardly noticed. She had fidgeted around, her

9

face losing the serenity that was her greatest asset. Something was bothering her. And Ann, busy peeping into the oven, stirring this, lowering the gas under that, hadn't noticed at first.

When she did notice Felicity's preoccupation, her cousin had started talking, and what she had to say had hit Ann like a blow. Ann remembered saying, her voice coming from a long way off, 'Are you telling me we're going to move? Just when we've settled? But why, why? And why didn't you say anything to me about it before now?'

Felicity had said awkwardly, 'I knew you weren't listening. No, not *we* – not exactly. Oh, this is so difficult! Listen Ann – *darling* – I got the chance to have this absolutely super flat with this other girl at my office, so I had to snap it up, didn't I? I mean, she's just my type – likes parties and staying up late and things like that! Confess it, Ann, parties simply aren't your scene, you know they aren't!'

Well, they might not be, but Ann had done all the cooking and preparation for past parties and not grumbled at the late hours nor the cleaning up the next morning. Somehow she hadn't been able to see what the argument was about or why Felicity should have been hinting that Ann was somehow to blame. She had said, bewildered, 'So ... you want me to find someone to share this flat with me so that Mrs Tate won't be cross at losing rent, is that it?' Mrs Tate wasn't all that bad as landladies went, but she did tend to get rather het up if a flat was not fully occupied, and told a long hard-luck tale about not being able to afford to lose even one person's rent for even one week.

Felicity hadn't answered but had merely looked frustrated.

'Well, if I can't find someone else, I don't mind paying double rent for one week,' Ann had faltered. 'Out of my savings. I mean, we've got this just as we wanted it and it's near my job and...' but Felicity cut in sharply.

Felicity lost her extraordinary prettiness when she was fussed and irritable as she had been then. 'Ann, darling Ann, you simply aren't *with it* and something's burning!' which again distracted Ann, but her cousin's next words sharply brought her back to listen more attentively. 'The whole thing is this is a *swap* arrangement. Two other girls want this place and if they don't get it, I can't go in with Tania. I don't know why or what the connection is. I didn't ask. It was a chance of a lifetime for me and there it is.'

Ann's clear eyes had regarded her cousin thoughtfully, trying to fit this all together, wondering how she had managed to share a flat with a girl who was, even if only distantly, related to her, and not known that

11

all this was being quietly arranged, to be burst on Ann at the last minute. Felicity had fidgeted, not liking the way things were going, and said at last, rather breathlessly, a little wheedling, 'Well, you wouldn't want me to have turned it down, and be stuck here in this dreary little hole for ever, would you? It's different for you – you manage to adapt, anywhere. But my job's so different. I'll never get on in my world without a good address – you must see that! And that's what Tania's flat is – a very good address!'

The words had jumbled all around in Ann's head, but all she had been able to think of just then was what her grandmother had once said about Felicity, who was, after all, a fifth-time removed cousin, and therefore not *close* in the old lady's eyes. 'Get that girl in a corner and she'll fight you like a little rat!' Gran had said. 'She's a Me-first girl, so you look out, Ann, or she'll trample all over you in order to get out first!'

Gran wasn't there any more. None of the relatives were. Ann was alone except for Felicity, and she had tended to regard Felicity as perhaps closer family than she should have done. She had protested to Gran at the time, saying, 'Not Felicity, Gran! She's so nice!' but Gran hadn't even bothered to answer that.

Looking at Felicity in utter bewilderment, Ann had said, 'So what have you arranged for me? Where will I go?'

Felicity in her turn had looked completely blank, as if the mere thought of fixing something for Ann, simply didn't come into it. She had quickly recovered, of course, saying briskly to Ann, 'As if I would insult you by fixing anything up for you, my dear! You're such a capable person – a *home* girl, if you see what I mean – and Rob-down-the-road is always looking yearningly at you. I just took it for granted that you'd want to get yourself something for the time being, and that you'd be married in no time at all and off to a place of your own.'

'But Rob's only a friend, nothing more,' Ann had protested faintly, shocked that such a viewpoint should have been considered. Felicity had seemed in that moment a stranger, an uncaring stranger who manoeuvred other people to get somewhere fast. That was the point when Ann discovered the chill in her stomach. It was there still. The chill that came with the thought of no roof over one's head. Other girls had a family they could run back to when things like this happened, but Felicity wouldn't understand that; she had never been a home girl. Perhaps she dimly realised that the elderly aunts and Gran had not really liked her. Ann knew Felicity had openly despised their lack of cash, their little economies, the fact that they merely rented their homes, and had very little that actually belonged to them. People who grew all their own vegetables, had hens in the back garden, and wore clothes for utility and not for fashion, were not people that Felicity understood or even liked.

Ann remembered saying, 'I must live near my job, because of the fares,' but Felicity had said in an exasperated tone, 'Do stop flapping about that job, Ann darling! It isn't a highly specialised one like mine. You could get another like it any day. You're the sort of girl who falls on her feet in a jiffy because you don't have to have high speed training and you're cosy, good at making people comfortable. Don't worry! You'll find someone needs someone like you, this very minute.' And because Ann had looked so sceptical at that viewpoint, Felicity had said in a challenging way, 'Just pick up that evening paper and look down the ads and you'll see how right I am! Gosh, look at the time, I must rush. Yes, I'm going out! Didn't I tell you? I *must* have!'

'But I've cooked all this food. I thought you said you were bringing a friend home,' Ann had protested, looking at the saucepans just ready to spoil their contents on the stove.

'Oh, sorry, yes – it fell through. Something else came up. Don't worry, ask Tom Westbury in from next door. He's always hungry. Or Rob down the road. What a slowtop you

14

are! Here's the chance of a lifetime, tempting some poor man with your good food! And all you can do is to stand there and look as if the sky's falling in.'

Ann closed her eyes on the changing scenery outside the train windows. Those moors were so much like her own miserable thoughts and that was where her new resident job was, on moors like those. 'What had she done?' she asked herself feverishly.

But there it was. She had been almost mesmerised into picking up that evening paper the minute Felicity, having rushed through a scented shower and got into her evening clothes at breakneck speed, shot through the flat with a gay, uncaring wave of the hand, supremely unconscious of the havoc she had raised in Ann's thudding heart. To be jobless, homeless, alone in the world, all in a few minutes, with the inevitability that had been written all over Felicity's pretty face, was a terrible thing. And there, in the personal column, as if Felicity had already seen it (which Ann doubted because Felicity wasn't interested enough to look for a job for someone else!) was this advertisement:

WANTED: FOR A RATHER SPECIAL RESIDENT JOB IN CORNWALL THAT CAN ONLY BE EXPLAINED IN COR-RESPONDENCE, YOUNG WOMAN, STRONG, HOMELY, WILLING TO

UNDERTAKE CARE OF SCHOOLGIRL RECUPERATING. STATE QUALIFA-CATIONS, SALARY AND WHEN FREE. *MUST HAVE BEEN RECENTLY JILTED.*

Looking back, Ann had to concede that the words 'resident job' had leapt out at her. Cornwall had struck her next, and after that in importance, the fact that the applicant must be young, strong, homely, and willing to undertake care of a schoolgirl. Following that order came the fact (with some relief) that she could say she was free at once.

The last sentence, which should have hit her first, only penetrated well after she had written and posted her letter of application.

A reply had come almost by return of post, as if they were waiting to snap up any applicant. Any qualms she may have had in the meantime were stilled by the fact that it was a woman writing. She sounded a comfortable motherly soul, said she believed it sounded just what was required, and that Ann must now attend in person for an interview, although that would be just a formality. Ann Ashley seemed to be just the person they needed. A single train ticket was enclosed, and the writer signed herself 'Mary Farraker'.

Well, maybe it did sound all right, but it wasn't all right. Ann felt it, deep inside her. It had been a desperate gamble, and of course they would not expect her to do anything else but stay. She had arranged for her trunk to follow her, because superstition wouldn't let her take it with her. What would she do if they didn't like her appearance or manner? But something was wrong and her heart had told her that, or why else had she refrained from showing Felicity the advertisement? True, Felicity hadn't pressed to see it. She had looked with some relief at the hole it had been cut out from in her evening paper, and she had said vaguely, 'Oh, good! You see? I knew you wouldn't make trouble ... what I mean is, I knew you'd land on your feet okay and I wouldn't have to worry over you.'

Ann supposed she had looked a bit indignant at that speech, for Felicity had said with sweet reason, 'Well, let's face it, it hasn't always been easy, has it, when I've wanted to lay on a quick party and you've been planning on going to bed early for a quiet time with a good book?' and she had managed to make Ann sound a definite drawback. 'By the way, what happened to all the food you were cooking?' Felicity had asked suddenly.

'Tom Westbury came looking for you and he was hungry,' Ann said vaguely, and Felicity had frowned and let the subject drop. She didn't want Tom Westbury's attentions. It wasn't really convenient having a doting next-door neighbour who popped out at the

17

sound of one's footsteps on the stairs or wanted to walk one to the bus in the morning if it was raining. Sharing his man's-size umbrella wasn't Felicity's idea of fun or romance. Neither was it her idea to have to listen to his dreams of 'getting up the ladder' and his dejected moods could be a decided embarrassment.

Ann didn't bother to enlarge on the matter of food, either. The fact that Tom had gone off with a portion of Ann's meat pie, and a wedge of her special meringue flan, to eat by the side of his typewriter, was neither here nor there. He would have drooled on and on about Felicity if Ann had invited him in to have the food with her, and that night she was just too depressed to listen. Besides, the rest of the food Ann had decided to take to the family whose ever-hungry members seemed to be bursting out of the walls of their flat at the back of the row in which Ann lived. Looking out of her window at their place, she was continually worried about them. They were delighted with the left-overs and called it a feast. Ann herself had lost her appetite.

Would she ever get it back again, she asked herself? Now, as her destination neared, it seemed to grow in importance, that last requirement in the advertisement. Why must the applicant have been jilted? Nobody had so far evinced the need to become engaged to Ann, let alone of jilting her. What on earth could she do about it now? Say she hadn't even noticed it, she had been wanting a resident job so badly? Or should she invent a man who had once wanted to marry her? But that last thing was beyond her. And then, in the pressure of other thoughts, such as why she should have been snapped up without any recommendation, or even a photo, she forgot the bit about being jilted.

Other thoughts nagged at her. Suppose she didn't like this Mrs Farraker, whose schoolgirl daughter needed a young strong woman to look after her while she recuperated … recuperated from what? And why must the applicant be strong? The modest amount she had decided to state as salary might be considered as too much, or on the other hand they might wonder why she had not asked for more. Worry ate into her soul so that she almost missed the Halt, except that Oldbridge was a biggish place, with a prize-winning set of flower beds of which the porters were inordinately proud. They shouted loud and clear which station it was.

Someone should meet her here, Ann hazily remembered, as she smoothed down her skirt, and wished that the jacket was only half as smart as Felicity's.

And then most of her troubles were swept

away by one of the porters who came up looking for her and asked in broad local dialect whether she was for Kingsbride. He repeated it. 'Kingsbride, the home of Mr Howard Crayne,' he said, as if that meant something. Ann, who only knew of a Mrs Farraker, said so, and wondered what could have gone wrong, but the porter nodded cheerfully. 'That's right, m'dear, that's the housekeeper. Said you was to be on this train. There's the car. We'll have this little ole case over in no time,' and he humped the one piece of Ann's luggage on to his shoulder and walked her out to where, in the cobbled yard, a dignified if old-fashioned Rolls stood waiting to collect her.

'Burridge, he do be powerful deaf,' the porter informed her, thereby cutting from Ann's feet the newly formulated plan of getting more information about her new home from the driver of the big car. So she sat back and looked at the scenery, which was hill, rough moorland, peppered at intervals with great veined white rocks as if some bored giant had flung them there and left them to get embedded in the soil. Bleak, lost, lonely, with only the sight of the washed out grey-blue sea, misty on its rim, to remind her that this was the end of England, a long way away from London, and those she had always known. All right for a holiday with one's return ticket

20

comfortably in one's purse. But she had no return ticket, and the job would have to be very bad for her to refuse it. This was her roof, her meal-ticket, her sheet-anchor, she thought miserably.

And then suddenly she had her first sight of Kingsbride.

It cuddled into a fold of the low hills; an unplanned rambling great house, of cold white-grey local stone, too many windows winking in the watery sunshine, like so many eyes eagerly looking out for the new-comer.

As they neared the place, the house rose up, revealing tidy yet extensive grounds behind wrought-iron gates. Tall gates, that made Ann think of being locked in ... or locked out. The thought made her shiver and it was a long time before she lost it, but it kept recurring. It was a thought that wouldn't be dislodged over the weeks and months. Not in a lifetime, she thought frenziedly.

Yet the inside of Kingsbride was warm and cosy enough. There were great fires built against the chill of the day, but not a dog or a flower in the place. Ann, who had filled the flat with blooms bought with her own money instead of buying herself small luxuries, had secretly yearned for a pet of her own. If not a dog, then a little cat. But here surely, animals were necessary? It was so lost and alone!

Yet Mrs Farraker's welcome was warm enough. She talked just like she wrote; comfortably, briefly, yet with the sound of someone who was glad that Ann had come.

'It's not entirely for me to say, of course, my dear, but if I was to be asked, I would say that you would suit right down to the ground,' and she led Ann up countless flights of shallow polished wooden stairs, where slender banisters were carved into figurines holding out arms which touched, forming the hand rail. Banisters that were probably old, hand-carved, and worth a great deal of money, as was the beautiful carved panelling. Ann's pursuits, as Felicity was always irritably pointing out, had a dead-end air about them, so far as finding men-friends, but were nevertheless likely to come in useful now, for from her browsing into great books in the reference library she could pick out periods and types of carving and panelling, place almost to the year the design of the fan-vaulting of the ceiling, and look with keen appreciation at the glory of the stained glass windows. Kingsbride was a period place, a thing of beauty, though hardly Ann's idea of a cosy home for a man to return to at the end of the day.

A man? There had been no mention of a man, had there, until at last the porter had told her the name of the owner of all this. An elderly man whose word was law, had been Ann's swift thought, and she had hoped devoutly that she wouldn't cross his path. She said, 'How old is the schoolgirl I am to look after?'

'Just eleven,' Mrs Farraker said, and subtly her tone had changed. Now there was a withdrawal, and the cosy welcome was sliding away. 'Opal Guinevere, she is called. So she will tell you and you can believe that.'

'Well, I would believe what the child told me, wouldn't I?' Ann said in some surprise, and received no answer. With a name like that, she would be growing up to be a beauty, Ann thought swiftly. Perhaps like Felicity. Gran had always said that a name rubbed off on a person. Rob down the road was therefore plain, thick-set and strong, as his name suggested. Tom next door had been lean and wiry, but strong just the same, and both young men had been plain no-nonsense types. Most of the stylish male friends of Felicity had had names to go with them. So Ann swiftly imagined that Opal Guinevere would already be tall, dignified, with the start of tender beauty, like the oil paintings she caught glimpses of as she ascended this beautiful staircase. She would also have a wonderful suite of rooms, with a special room for the nurse, if her health was frail.

They kept on until yet another floor of the great house was reached. Now the panelling had been left behind. Everything up here was plain, no nonsense; the servants' quarters? Ann looked in surprise at the housekeeper, who said swiftly, 'We have so many rooms up here, and the master he do like his peace and quiet and the young lady is not really what you might call peaceful. So we have put her at the end and fixed up a room for you to be with her, miss, but you'll be comfortable. It's comfortable if not stylish.'

The story of my life, Ann thought ruefully: comfortable but not stylish. Oh, well, what else had she really expected? And they turned a corner and opened yet another door. The plain doors up here were no less heavy and close shutting, able to muffle any noise, Ann could see. But it wasn't so comfortable, looking out on the tops of the trees, with the wild moors stretching eternally seawards beyond them. The wind would whip in from the sea and catch the roof and upper storeys, with little to protect it, Ann thought, and while she was pondering on this, a thin child in faded jeans and a grubby tee-shirt, lounged round the corner and leaned against the wall, staring at them.

Her thin, peaky face was dirty, too, and her hands had caked mud on them. Her eyes looked owlishly out from round spectacles, and her hair looked as if it had been chopped with dress-making scissors by someone who had had no hairdressing experience at all.

The housekeeper made annoyed sounds under her breath, but before she could begin to explain or introduce anyone, the child said, 'Hello! You my new keeper? I'm a prisoner, you know.'

TWO

'Miss Opal!' the housekeeper exclaimed, and turned to Ann, distressed. 'Oh, well, I never did! And I left her neat and clean in a decent blue dress with a clean white collar and cuffs and *now* look at her! Nothing much can be done about that hair – she hacked it off herself, only yesterday, but there! You've seen her like this so you know what you have to expect. A lot of washing, scrubbing and struggling goes on, before meal-times, I don't mind telling you.'

She turned back to Ann, and was outraged to see Ann's soft mouth curling up in a smile of pure amusement. Ann remembered only too well how Felicity as a child had ripped off 'clothes for the visitor' and got into as dirty a state as she could, just to shock everyone. 'It's comfortable like that, I expect,' she said.

Opal's mouth fell open. After a moment she exploded, 'You're supposed to be furious and threaten to go back to London!'

Ann smiled at Mrs Farraker. 'If this is my charge, I think we shall do very well together.'

But the likeness to Felicity when young,

finished there. Opal felt let down, so she went into a sulk and wouldn't speak. Ann decided that the worst possible situation was to try and talk to someone who was unwilling to answer, and nothing was helped by Mrs Farraker being with them, conducting a stiff meal-time in what was called the day nursery.

'When will I have my interview?' Ann asked her.

It seemed that there was to be no interview. 'The master left it to me to choose a suitable applicant, someone *I* could get along with,' Mrs Farraker said, picking her words with care. 'And I like what I've seen of you, so if you are willing to take the job on, shall we arrange for the rest of your luggage to be brought from the station?'

'There haven't been any other people wanting the job,' Opal said clearly, which made the housekeeper go poppy red and look angrily at the child, who was cheekily regarding the ceiling.

'I left my trunk at my old address,' Ann broke in swiftly, 'not being sure if I'd be suitable. I'll write and ask for it to be sent on,' so Mrs Farraker with some relief showed Ann the rest of the small domain that would be hers and the child's and prepared to leave her.

'Won't I be expected to see the master at all?' Ann asked.

Mrs Farraker said, 'When he comes back. He's away at the moment.' She looked severely at the child. 'I know you've been ill, miss, but you're better now, and you must remember your manners and say "Miss Ashley".'

They watched Mrs Farraker depart to the lower regions. She was a thickset woman with a comfortable way of speaking and a cheerful likeable face until it alighted on Opal. Ann was puzzled.

But that point could be cleared up later. Meantime communication must be established between herself and this bright child with the unfortunate lack of good looks. So when the housekeeper's footsteps had faded at last into the distance and Ann and Opal stood in silence where she had left them, Ann grinned at the child and said, 'I say, can we really make as much noise up here as we like and nobody hear us anywhere else?'

Opal was startled and regarded her severely. 'You're not supposed to be a sport. You have to find me very difficult, so I can make a fuss and then you'll be asked to go, just like the others.'

'The others? But I thought you said there had been nobody else?'

'Not with this last advert in the newspaper. We had two people before, and each one couldn't stand Uncle Howard no-how and went. What's "jilted" mean?'

'Jilted!' Ann exclaimed and wondered how she was going to get out of that one. 'Why do you want to know? Where did you hear it?'

Opal regarded her, then decided to answer those questions. 'The first governess we had said that jilted or no jilted, if she'd known what Uncle Howard wanted, she wouldn't have come within miles of the place. And the next one said that if that was why he wanted a jilted person, he ought to be put away!'

'Oh, I can't think they'd say things like that about your guardian,' Ann urged, but her heart was beating faster, and the sense of being entrapped was even greater than when she had been driven through those tall wrought iron gates. This wouldn't do, she scolded herself. She must get to the bottom of this. 'What's your guardian like?' she asked. 'You must tell me if you can, because it's important.'

Opal shot a sly sideways glance at her, and swung experimentally from the mantel-piece, trying not very successfully to scorch the end of her jeans, as she said, 'He's got a lump on his back, and you have to pretend you don't see it, or he'll hit you with his knobbly walking stick. He's very old and nasty and the people in the kitchen say his father was raving mad and got shut up in the West Tower only they couldn't undo the lock on the door so he died of fright.'

'Now just a minute,' Ann said indignantly, after the first wash of fear had ebbed away before common sense. 'I can't possibly believe all that stuff!'

'I'm only telling you what the people in the kitchens say,' Opal said innocently. 'I don't know of course, what went on in the West Tower, now do I? But I do know about the lump on Uncle's back. Why is it called being a hunchback?'

That had the sound of sweet reason about it. Ann felt a little queer. Why hadn't she been warned? Then she braced herself. Why should she mind what the poor man looked like? It was probably the only reason why the others hadn't stayed, thereby leaving open the job for Ann herself, who needed one so badly. She could discount, she thought, his beating her – the child obviously loved exaggerating – but that he was possibly not straight in the back probably accounted for his not showing himself to every newcomer. Perhaps she would never see him! She held on to that thought.

Meantime Opal watched her covertly, then reminded her, 'You promised you'd say what jilting meant.'

Ann had had to deal with children before. Remembering the noisy though lovable bunch who lived near the flat and who had helped demolish the food she had cooked for that last party that hadn't happened, she said seriously, 'It means losing the chance of a very good place.'

She kept a perfectly straight face as Opal's eyes behind the spectacles searched her own. The child was obviously disappointed. 'Then why do they say "poor thing" then? They did when Winnie in the kitchen got jilted last November.'

'Well, I don't know the circumstances, do I? Why do you want to know?'

'Because the people in the kitchen were talking about the people who come to look after me and I wanted to know why they must be jilted first. I thought it meant being beaten with a big ash stick like Uncle Howard's.'

'No, it means having lost the chance, they snap up this new one very quickly,' Ann said, resolving to find out at the first opportunity how it was that this child knew, from all this way away from the kitchens, what the people down there were saying, and why so much gossip was allowed anyway.

Perhaps some of it showed in her face, for Opal said quickly, 'And I must tell you not to try to go down to the kitchens and find out for yourself, because they've got a … a monster down there. Truly!'

'A – what?' Ann gasped. 'Oh, now, come along, this really won't do. Where do we have our evening meal, because I think it would be nice to make a party of it, if I can possibly persuade someone to let me have a little portable stove up here. I'm a pretty good cook, you know, unless of course you like Mrs Farraker's cooking best? We could just have things cooked for special tea, I thought.'

'No, every meal,' Opal said quickly. 'Because Mrs Farraker gets cross with me. You saw her. And when she's cross, she won't let any food be brought up to me. That's why I got ill before. You just don't know what goes on here!'

Ann looked at Opal steadily, then the child scuffed the floor with her toe and admitted, 'Well, sometimes she doesn't.' Then in a burst of confidence she added, 'Nobody likes me, that's the thing! You'll find out!' and while Ann was conceding to herself that Mrs Farraker had looked at the child with no great liking, Opal ruined the whole effect by saying experimentally, 'The thing is, there's some sort of mystery about my birth. Nobody likes mysteries, especially at Kingsbride.'

Ann sighed. The child was lonely, unsure of herself, she told herself. In a way, as she had said to the housekeeper, Opal was very like herself at that age; misunderstood, craving warmth and companionship and not finding any. She put an arm round the child's shoulders and briefly squeezed her to her own side; an odd, almost boyish gesture that Opal didn't object to at all, and said, 'Yes, well, Opal, I think you and I understand each other, don't we?'

The child exaggerated, that was what it was. She lived in a make-believe world. Ann shrugged, and began to settle in with the few things she had. And later, when she had the chance to discuss the new cooking arrangements with Mrs Farraker and found that august lady more than willing to have a small stove brought up, if only to 'save the legs of the staff, such as it was', they seemed to be on better relations all round. With that in mind, Ann was moved to say delicately, 'How much can I believe of what Opal says?'

'Oh, not a thing, my dear! The child's just a little liar, everyone knows that!'

'Then I can discount everything she says about her guardian?' Ann pressed.

'That I wouldn't like to say,' the housekeeper said. 'But anyway, you'll be seeing him for yourself and you can form your own opinion, but this I will say – whatever he looks like, to you, wait till you find out what he's like as a man, underneath. The outside doesn't matter, in my opinion.'

Ann's heart sank. So that, of course, would be true, about his being a hunchback. But everything else she could discount, including the Monster in the kitchen and the gossip that went on there, and the reasons why the other two young women had left. But before she could hold this idea long enough to take any comfort from it, the housekeeper said reluctantly, 'There is one thing. If Opal ever mentions a mystery about her birth, I think you should discourage that right away. You see,' and she looked round quickly as if expecting the walls to have ears, 'I don't know – I don't think anyone knows – just what that child's position in this family is. And you can't ask.'

'But I thought she was the ward of Mr Crayne, although sometimes she refers to him as her uncle,' Ann put in quickly, anxious to get it right.

The housekeeper shook her head. 'I just don't know. Nobody knows. And it would be out of the question for you to try and find out. The Craynes are a very proud family. Especially old Mrs Crayne.'

'Old Mrs Crayne?' Ann frowned. It was the first she had heard of such a person. Was this the wife of the man who died in the tower?

'Oh, yes, my dear, you will be seeing her as soon as she is fit enough. As a matter of fact, the arrangement was that in Mr Howard's absence, his mother should discuss your position (that's if you suited in all else) and the special arrangements, but the fact is, Mrs Crayne does enjoy such poor health, and I must say she has had a very nasty cold all this week. I'm not surprised you weren't sent for her to see her.'

'But why should I be sent for?' Ann asked.

'Why, it all centres round the child, come to think of it. Certainly, it's this special thing about the child's birth. I don't know if anything will be said about it. I doubt it very much. There'll be too much else to discuss and arrange, I'm sure. No, much the best, my dear, if we pretend, although we know perfectly well otherwise, that there certainly is no mystery about Opal's birth.'

It was a pouring wet day when Ann was sent for to go to the rooms of old Mrs Crayne. It boded no good. Already, although she had been there just over a week, Ann had started to imbibe the special superstitions of Cornwall, particularly this remote part of the moors. And there were many superstitions, and every place had a special name, with a story behind it. Opal was only too ready to tell her the stories, and when Ann checked them with other people, they were always a little wild, rather wide of the mark but essentially right, like a story that has been handed down and got a little warped in the telling.

Mrs Crayne was not so old as Ann had been led to believe. A well-preserved sixty, with a fine skin, unwrinkled, and the remains of what must have been extremely good looks in her youth. Her white hair was beautifully dressed, and the masses of rings and bracelets she wore, confirmed Ann's first impression that old Mrs Crayne was extremely proud of her hands. She wore such up-to-the-minute clothes that Ann at once felt dowdy, and looking round the elegant apartment, Ann began to put names to the treasures there, from the cabinet of Sèvres porcelain, to the Aubusson carpet, the tapestry hangings that must have been hand-worked in the thirteenth century, to the fine crystals hanging from the central lighting. All this in a first glance that still didn't cloud her wits, so that Ann was also aware of a curious enmity beneath the pleasant manner of Howard Crayne's mother. But how could this woman hate her, since she hardly knew her, and Ann was, after all, no more than one of the staff?

The soft blue of the beautifully designed gown accentuated the blue of Mrs Crayne's eyes, but they still mirrored hostility that even the friendly pat by one of those beautiful hands on a seat near her, couldn't take away. Mrs Crayne said, 'I am sorry, my dear, that I have been too indisposed to see you before now. I did promise my son, but to be frank, I still feel far too unwell to do all that he wished me to in this interview. He is a very capable man and I am sure he will be able to conduct this interview in half the time. But there is no reason why you should not tell me about yourself.'

Mrs Crayne was a person who put a quiet little question here, a deliberate controversial suggestion there, to get a quick denial and the answer that might not perhaps have been forthcoming otherwise. Ann remembered how Gran had roundly condemned the sort of person who 'said the wrong to get the right'. Ann, who had been at once aware that she, too, felt a rising dislike of this elegant woman, promised herself that she would give little away, but in no time at all, it seemed, Mrs Crayne was in possession of the fact that Ann now had nobody except an attractive cousin who had edged her out of their shared flat, and that Ann now had no roof over her head and very little money saved. It made Ann feel very vulnerable, as if this woman was pleased to think that Ann was so completely dependent on this family for everything, as indeed she was. But not a thing did she disclose that Ann wanted to know, even when Ann asked for information, such as the relationship between them and the child.

'I merely wondered if my guesswork was correct – she is only adopted, perhaps, and doesn't know that? It is important for me to know.'

Mrs Crayne frowned on such an idea. 'It makes little difference to you what her background is, unless my son decides to tell you,' she said smoothly. 'So far as is necessary, you must know that the child is alone very much and needs someone to look after her, be a companion as well as to see that she doesn't re-develop her illness...'

'I don't know yet what that illness was, Mrs Crayne.'

'She's a little chesty, but the doctors make much of it,' Mrs Crayne said definitely. 'See that she doesn't get in a draught or stay out in the wet or the cold, and that she eats a good plain diet and gets plenty of exercise and sleep. An hour before midnight is worth two afterwards, and good Cornish fresh air is worth a dozen doctors.' Mrs Crayne said all that with an air of having made a pronouncement of wisdom that was worth its weight in gold, and Ann realised that she was being dismissed on that note.

She got to her feet automatically but as a last resort, she said, 'But Mrs Crayne, are you aware that if Opal doesn't want to eat, she won't?'

'You must see, by fair means or foul, that she does,' Mrs Crayne said gravely, and waved a hand in a gesture of dismissal that couldn't be ignored.

As the door closed on Ann, an inner door opened and Mrs Crayne's companion emerged, her eyes raised interrogatively to see if she was wanted. She was also Mrs

Crayne's maid and confidante. Mrs Crayne looked at her now with raised eyebrows.

'Did you get a sight of her?' she asked.

Her companion nodded.

'Well, Gertrude, what did you think of her? And what do you think my son will think of her when he sees her?'

The companion was a good ten years younger than her mistress but knew which side her bread was buttered. She was thinking that Ann had a rather 'taking' personality, a disposition that was earnest, one that wouldn't be thwarted by people or things, and that on the whole she was a young woman likely to be more comfortable to have around than either of the other two who had been tried in the job. But clearly Howard Crayne's mother didn't want to hear that, so Gertrude said diplomatically, 'I don't think she'll do, I don't think she'll do at all, Mrs Crayne.'

'And why not, Gertrude?' Mrs Crayne asked, but she looked quietly pleased. 'How would you describe her to me if I hadn't seen her?'

'Rather ordinary, madam. No colouring to speak of. Certainly not one who will be able to do much for Miss Opal, but that is only my opinion, of course.' And in her heart she thought that Opal might do very well to have someone like Ann Ashley to go into battle with. Gertrude had already heard some of the conversations Ann had had with the child. A clever way with a child that age, that Ann had. But it didn't make any difference what was said in this room to this woman, Gertrude thought, remembering the scenes there had been between Howard Crayne and his mother in the recent past. If Howard approved of this girl, nothing his mother could do would shift her. If only the girl had the stamina to stand up to Opal's tiresome disposition, and the intrigues the old lady might start.

They discussed Howard Crayne's needs in a desultory way, his mother setting them out as she thought they should be set out, and the companion murmuring agreement as she unpicked a difficult piece of knitting her mistress had abandoned, made the correction and quietly put it near those beautiful hands, without saying a word. It wouldn't do to let Mrs Crayne think her muddled knitting had been noticed or taken such pains to put right. She always told people, especially the vicar's wife, that she was a very advanced knitter and designed all the things she sent to the Church Bazaar.

'My son Howard must not be worried,' his mother said. 'There has been enough worry in the past.'

Gertrude agreed.

'And if everyone had listened to me, that nice Minerva wouldn't have gone off and married that vulgarly rich man Thornton, who was no good to her and has now got himself killed in some stupid accident and left her all alone. Such a beautiful girl and so clever at everything. She should have been the chatelaine of Kingsbride.'

Gertrude said firmly that that was the only conviction worth considering, but all the time her thoughts were going round in a maze. Why had Mrs Crayne mentioned Minerva Thornton on this particular day? If she kept very quiet, would Gertrude now hear the whole story behind that stormy engagement that had been broken so shatteringly only a few short years ago? And would Mrs Crayne reveal why her son had that streak of white in the raven black of his hair? A streak of white above a high forehead lent him even more distinction, Gertrude privately thought, but she wasn't envious of the beautiful girls who were paraded before the terribly strong and almost always angry Howard Crayne. She was glad she was middle-aged and only a companion. This was a more or less secure job and she could creep away when the people in her employer's family were having high words. It was like a mouse burrowing in its nest while lightning and thunder rolled round the skies. Keep out of sight and those above wouldn't even notice you were there.

But, Gertrude wondered, with a warming

of the heart as she thought of her, what would that girl Ann do? Not a shred of beauty about her, yet there was a graciousness, a warm glow in that quiet face, and a charm and dignity in the plain utilitarian clothes and the neatly dressed hair that was such a pale brown, yet when it was caught in the sun's slanting rays and the top seemed to shimmer as if just a few hairs were gold, Gertrude had noticed that that neat head then had more charm than the mistress's troublesome hair sets. Much more satisfactory than the rather artificial blonde of Minerva Thornton's hair, she remembered, although Minerva had been to such an expensive hairdresser to get it. Much more taking than the redhead who had held Ann's job so briefly before her, whose wild colouring had so much upset that tiresome son of the housekeeper's. Gertrude paused to wonder how it was that the housekeeper had been allowed to keep him there. She supposed vaguely that it was because he was so strong for carrying things, and he did no harm, that was such a comfort.

'You must keep me informed of how things go between that young woman and Opal Guinevere,' Mrs Crayne suddenly said, in a fretful voice which reminded Gertrude that the time was near for her special job of brewing the fine tea, half China, which her mistress loved. She rose quietly to her feet, but now there was something of great interest to speed her through the mundane tasks of every day. What would happen when Howard Crayne returned and met that girl? Somehow Gertrude didn't think Ann would be sent away like the others.

Ann knew nothing of Gertrude, her years of service or her devotion to the Crayne family. She learned new names and faces one by one, as if reluctantly the housekeeper allowed them to be divulged. It was no use asking the housekeeper outright about anything. Ann had early discovered that. A quiet person herself, Ann went about her cooking on the little stove found for her, and won part approbation from young Opal because certain meals a day could be regarded as fun, 'indoor picnics' as she called them. The housekeeper was favourably impressed, and as a kind of reward for the child's appetite being tempted, she trickled out the information that the big young man who said little but did the heavy jobs about the place was her son, and that his name was Jago. Ann, in her first flush of victory in getting this much information from the woman, was immediately dashed by Mrs Farraker begging her not to mention him nor to speak to him if she saw him. 'Shy, rare shy, he is, but strong, and such a good useful boy to me, to everyone.'

After the housekeeper had left their

quarters, Opal, who as always had been eavesdropping, said bluntly, 'He's the Monster I told you about.' But before Ann's frowning look of mounting anger, Opal decided to leaven his information with truth, so that in the end Ann didn't know what to believe: 'Oh, well, perhaps not a Monster, but he's what the girls from the village call "Not-All-There",' and try as she would, Ann couldn't help wondering how she was going to stick this job out.

The whispering night wind over the moors, the sound of the moaning from the sea, the slow hiss and the crash of returning tide, were all new sounds to a town dweller; now this information about someone in the house who was a little odd, worried her anew. Perhaps she might not have felt so uneasy if she hadn't been told how big and strong he was. She said firmly to Opal, 'I think I shall stop picnic meals every time you tell me something that isn't the truth. It isn't fair. I'm doing my best to get you fit and well. You might be a sport and not worry me with stories like that!'

'But it's true, it's true! I tell you what–' Opal said with a little rush, 'never mind what they say about me not going out in the rain. Let's go out for a walk on the moors all wrapped up, the next time the wind blows in all wet from the sea, and you'll see Jago busy out there.'

'Busy? Doing what, for goodness' sake?'

'Oh, lots of things,' the child said vaguely, again filling Ann with suspicion. 'He collects driftwood…'

'But what would a great house like this need driftwood for?'

Opal looked slantingly at Ann, and tried out for size her latest outrageous remark. At least, Ann thought it was so. 'They're all hard up here because old Mrs Crayne spends a fortune on herself, so they economise by collecting driftwood. Oh, and he cuts peat, and they use seaweed…'

'Now really, Opal, that will do!' Ann said fiercely, and to set the child down a little, she stopped play for the rest of the day and laid on lessons. She had done this for the young child of a neighbour once, and although she wasn't trained to teach, her own love of books was enough for the purpose. She started with geography and they were both soon so immersed in the fascination of tracing maps and reading them, that they forgot it was time for the lamps. The housekeeper brought up two, and Ann was again amazed at this primitive form of lighting, acquired by pumping, that gave out such a bright yet soft light. But Opal's curiosity about map reading had been aroused against her will and for the rest of the evening she questioned Ann on the subject. So next day, when the walk on the moors was again broached by the child, Ann didn't feel she could reasonably say no.

Ann and Opal had found Jago in a hollow trying to catch something that moved with panic speed. Ann felt that upsurge of fear because Jago clearly wasn't quite like other people, but the child was in her care, so she braced herself to go forward, show nothing of her apprehension, and treat the giant as if he were quite normal. And after all, she discovered that the swift-moving thing was merely a bird with an injured leg. She asked Opal if she knew anything of first-aid for animals, and Opal said she didn't, and looked narrowly at Ann. Everything depended on Ann's courage or lack of it, now.

She shrank back behind Ann. 'Let's go the other way. That bird's going mad,' Opal pleaded.

'Nonsense,' Ann said briskly. 'It's in pain and afraid. Now, let's show Jago we mean to help him,' and she went forward confidently, smiling broadly at him and nodding at the bird. 'Opal, we three will make a triangle round it and we'll catch it that way. Well, I will, when it flies away from you.'

But it took time, first to reassure Jago and the dogs with him, then to keep catching the frightened hurt creature, which kept breaking away and hiding. But at last Jago caught on what they were meaning to do, and their swooping figures, with their clothes blown about in the wind, converged on the hurt creature, and must have looked weird to the onlooker. They were all three so intent on what they were doing that they didn't hear the big car purr to a standstill on the road a few yards off. Curiosity made the man in the car get out to investigate what three odd figures were doing popping up and down in such a way, in the hollow, their clothes flapping like dark wings.

He was no stranger to the district, so he recognised the largest figure at once, a fact which smartened his pace till he reached them. Nobody but Jago Farraker would wave his great arms above his head in such a lunatic fashion, and when he moved, he revealed a slim young woman whose wide grey eyes and pale face revealed such anxiety and distress, that he jumped to the erroneous conclusion that Jago had lost his grip and was attacking someone, a thing he had always secretly feared. He broke into a run towards the hollow, reaching it from behind them, startling all three of them just as they had caught the bird. His height loomed over them.

'What the devil do you think you're about?' he thundered, in a voice which to poor Jago meant certain punishment.

Jago dropped his arms and cowered low in the dip where they were: Ann, Opal, and an assortment of dogs and a puppy, and a great bird that Ann was trying to restrain from escaping in her cupped hands.

She had no idea who this thunderous browed dark young man could be, with the strong angry voice and the arrogant chin, but she did know that for some time – it seemed a long time though it wasn't really – she had patiently tried to understand what Jago had needed of her, and had succeeded, and besides coming near to winning his confidence, she had equally patiently tried to keep down Opal's excitement at being allowed out on such a windy day.

'Oh, please don't shout at him, you'll frighten him! Besides, he's doing no harm! Do you know anything about injured birds?' she demanded, thinking that the only person on the moor on such a day must be the vet, as she already knew the doctor was an elderly man.

Jago heard the question and partly understood it, and kept shaking his head at Ann and braving the stranger's ferocious frown to stand between Ann with the bird, and him. 'All right, Jago,' she said softly, 'don't worry. I'll mend his leg myself. If you can find me a twig. A little one. A strong one, if you can.'

Jago's face turned into one great huge smile and he nodded several times and stormed out of the hollow to do her bidding, which clearly filled him with pleasure.

'Help him, Opal, there's a good girl,' Ann said, in such an ordinary voice that Opal started to go and do as she said, when the stranger intervened sharply. 'No! What on earth are you doing out in weather like this anyway, young woman?' he demanded of the child. 'Go over to my car at once and stay there!'

Ann was furious and got to her feet, which wasn't easy since the bird with the hurt leg was struggling so madly. 'I don't know who you are,' she said angrily, 'a neighbour, I suppose. But Opal is in my charge and with me she stays. I brought her out, and I'll take her back. Besides, it's good for her to be out in the fresh air. She's well wrapped up and enjoying herself. Now please leave us!'

'Who the deuce are you to talk to me like that?' he demanded.

Opal looked wretchedly at Ann. She couldn't see for the damp on her glasses and it was all wrong that this should happen just when she was enjoying herself so much. They'd send Ann away and she would get into trouble for persuading the new person in charge of her to take her out in this kind of weather.

'I am in charge of Opal, who lives at Kingsbride, and Mrs Crayne knows all about it and…' Ann almost said 'approves' but since Mrs Crayne was never likely to approve of anything as far as Ann could see, she changed that to, 'Mrs Crayne has not been disapproving of the idea and you see how interested Opal is in things! You must see, since you appear to know her, what a change there is!'

'I do indeed,' he said grimly, and left them to march back to his car.

Opal muttered, 'I'll be beaten, I know I will. And Jago will be sent away and Mrs Farraker will get the sack and—'

'Stop that at once,' Ann said in a low voice, as she caught sight of Jago eagerly returning with his twigs. 'Don't ever let him hear you say such things. It will obviously upset him. Besides, we don't know there will be trouble, do we?'

Jago waited eagerly, sure that this determined, practical young woman would settle everything. He had never seen any woman grapple with a hurt bird before, but somehow he was sure Ann could do it. He watched her carefully, still not entirely sure of her, but he seemed to be able to understand her simple commands and requests and to do things as she wanted. And so he finally had the bird firmly held in his great hands, leaving Ann free to splint the broken leg with the twig, and a strip of sticky plaster from a small tin which she always carried about with her. Jago watched keenly as she strapped it together. Even the hurt creature seemed to know it was being made well, for now it had stopped struggling. At last, when Ann had done all she could, she let Jago take it, putting it under his coat. Then he stood looking at her worshipfully, while Opal uneasily looked on.

'That's all right, now, Jago. You can go now. Better take it home. Have you got a cage or something to keep it in?'

The reaction surprised her. He shook his head fiercely. 'No cage! No cage! Bird die in cage!'

Opal said under her breath, 'He keeps all his creatures in the utility rooms under the manor. Don't let his mother know!'

'Oh, I see. Shall I come and see the bird when it's better, Jago?' she asked him with her sweet smile, and he nodded his head excitedly. 'Off you go, then!'

He turned into the teeth of the wind, all his clothes flapping around him, and he looked like a huge animated scarecrow. Ann watched him, the dogs at his heels, but Opal was nervously looking back at the road.

'Look, the car didn't go after all. Oh, that man! I hate him! He's calling to us to get in.'

'But we can't!' Ann protested. 'We can't take a lift from a stranger. Well, *I* don't know him even if you do. Whatever next?'

'He's not a stranger,' Opal admitted reluctantly. She gulped. 'He's my guardian, Uncle Howard, come back early.'

Ann gasped as her reeling senses took in

that the handsome young man was her employer. 'But you said he was an old man, and a hunchback at that!' she said at last.

Opal burst into tears. 'I know I did. I do it to them all, tell fibs I mean, only now I wish I hadn't, because I like you and I don't want you to be sent away.'

'Well, after the way I spoke to him just now, I can't think I shall have any alternative!' Ann retorted.

THREE

Ann's first interview with her employer took place immediately on their return, predictably in the book room, a stone-floored room with austere shelving and dark musty tomes in sombre faded crimsons, browns and greens. The room smelt like a church, in spite of the big wood fire burning in the open hearth. She resentfully decided he had brought her to this room for the express purpose of making her feel more uncomfortable than she was. Actually it was a room he personally liked, and was aiming to do some work at the long table after he had dismissed her. To his masculine mind a room with a huge fire was the ideal room in which to discuss what they now had to talk over.

As Ann didn't even know the nature of this threatened talk and wrongly guessed it was about her unsuitability (or otherwise) to look after Opal, she looked stormily at him and was most unhelpful.

He studied her. From his great height she looked rather cute, being small made, small featured, a girl with soft colouring and a very nice voice. Voices were so important. Yes, she was a good type, but oh, so pugnacious. He wondered how she had got on with his mother. In fact, he had a good idea how that lady found Ann, since she had decided to be 'unwell' and therefore unable to see him although he had only just returned. Somebody in that elegant room of his mother's must have made the fur and feathers fly!

He smiled faintly at the thought, and invited Ann to sit down, a thing she couldn't do since she was sure she would be scolded, if not actually dismissed, for her part in that scene on the moor and she preferred to stand for a dressing-down.

'Very well, if you stand, then I shall have to, which is a nuisance, because I am cold, tired, and not very comfortable. I am actually very good-tempered considering how uncomfortable I am, and I'll go further – if there is anything you think I have done wrong or been unfair about, then I'll apologise now, before we continue. Now I can't be more magnanimous than that, surely?'

She wouldn't be appeased. She felt a fool. Somebody should have warned her that he was returning today. Somebody should have told her what he looked like, not led her to think he was a cross-patch deformed elderly man who was bossy most of the time and fairly unpleasant all of the time. But she couldn't say so, without risk of losing her job, and that incensed her further. She said stiffly, 'There is no need to apologise … sir … I was at fault.'

He stared. 'Good heavens, do we have to be so formal? You have had a talk with my mother about the requirements of this job, surely?' She nodded, still frostily, so believing the talk with his mother had been every bit as comprehensive as he said he wished it to be before he had gone away, he decided that he could take it from there. Mistakenly, as it happened, since the talk with his mother had been painfully brief, and hardly helpful on either side, as Ann recalled only too well. 'She doesn't like me, I think,' she said.

'I'm not surprised. Oh, I didn't mean that! What I meant was, my mother doesn't like anyone until she gets to know them and sometimes people feel they can't or won't wait that long.' He smiled at her, but in her present uncomfortable and unforgiving mood, it was the smile on the face of the tiger. She distrusted it whole-heartedly.

'You wanted to say something to me, sir?'

Now he was frankly nettled. 'Not *sir*. My name is Howard – you must have been told that, surely?'

Now surprise and indignation intermingled. 'I don't think I understand!' She jutted her chin and said, 'I need this job, sir, very badly, and I am trying to do it well. I understood that it was solely for the purpose of looking after Opal – nurse/companion/governess (although I have to admit I haven't been trained for the teaching part) but I did say so in the first letter, and after all, to get a child interested in what one has been reading on such subjects as history and geography, for a start, is surely something, until she can go away to a proper school?'

'That is the whole point. She isn't going away to school. You must have been told that!'

'If I have, I didn't fully understand it,' she flashed. 'What else am I supposed to have been told, that I didn't fully understand? I knew what I was doing today, taking her out well wrapped up. She's had a wonderful time and was thoroughly interested – thrilled to be out of the house!'

'I'm sure!' Now he was getting as frosty as Ann. 'But we are surely wandering from the point.' He decided to begin at the beginning. 'In the first instance, you contacted us ... how?'

'From an advertisement in the London evening newspaper I had.'

'Have you that advertisement with you at this moment?'

'No, but I can remember it, word for word.'

'Then oblige me by repeating it, will you?' he requested, in such a tone that she knew very well she couldn't refuse.

'I don't know why I must, sir. You know very well what you put in the advertisement, but this is what it said,' and she repeated the piece quite accurately.

He told her so. 'Now, to take it from there, what did you expect to be needed for, apart from your duties towards Opal? Don't stand there looking blank! I am referring to the last sentence, which is the point of the whole advertisement. You are, I presume, really jilted, and not secretly engaged to be married?'

'Oh, no, I'm not engaged,' she said, her heart beginning to flutter. There is was! Hadn't she known that no good would come of that beastly advertisement with its final sinister requirement?

'And you have really been jilted?' he insisted, so, during one shaken and fleeting but vital minute she had to make up her mind to tell a lie and keep this job, or tell the truth and lose it. The stark remembrance of a London night, cold and raining, with nowhere to go, made up her mind for her. She said breathlessly, 'Yes, I've been jilted,' and it was out. Moreover, it sounded true, to her astonished but ashamed ears.

Having said it, there was no more she could do about it. So much for her belief that these people would have the decency not to probe the wound and mention the thing after the jilted person had arrived!

Howard Crayne had no such delicacy of feeling, it seemed. 'Well, what were the circumstances?' he shocked her by demanding.

To be jilted, you had first to have been courted. Ann had never had such; an experience. She was the home girl, who sometimes obligingly had made up a fourth, so that the two men in the party could be switched, her cousin thereby getting the man she really did want, with Ann being left with the one that Felicity didn't want. And of course, there was no repeat date for that piece of work! The old blind date had been taken on, too, also at Felicity's request. But – not counting the shy smiles of Rob-down-the-road – that was all. So Ann decided to sound tight-lipped and sore about the whole thing and with a bit of luck he would realise he shouldn't be probing the wound and leave her alone.

'He didn't want me, so … there it ended,' she said.

'How had you offended the gentleman, if one may ask?' Howard pursued with heavy patience. 'And can we give him a name for easier reference?'

'Well, why do you want to know all this, sir?'

'It will soon be over, like a visit to the dentist. I just want to check its validity because we have already had one young lady here who invented a jilting so that she could try out the job. We didn't like that so we invited her to go and I imagine she wasn't sorry. As an experiment, it really hadn't suited either side.'

'But why do you want to know the truth? How does my affair of the heart concern my ability to look after Opal?'

'I have to know I can trust you, for a start. The name?'

He had got out a gold screw pencil from his pocket, and a workmanlike notebook in a leather case. Ann quailed before such heavy efficiency, and hastily called on the only man's name she could think of, on the spur of the moment. Tom Westbury in the flat next door.

'Tom. Thomas, I presume? Westbury.'

'No,' she said fiercely, 'what I said. Tom Westbury.'

'I see. And his address?'

She gave it tight-lipped. Why pursue this insane business? Was Howard Crayne intending to contact Tom and ask if he had really jilted Ann? Tom would come and demand to know why such things were being said about him. Oh, no, she thought, in sudden relief, Tom wouldn't be there. He was going for his holiday, she recalled, and straight on to a job that was taking him to Aberdeen for six months. There had been all that fuss because he had wanted Felicity to marry him and go to Scotland and she had indignantly refused.

Well, that might well be used by Ann herself as the reason for this, if this wretched Howard Crayne intended to pursue the reason, and of course, he did. 'So you decided that as you couldn't bear the thought of going to live in Aberdeen, you said so, loud and clear, and the gentleman didn't like it?'

'He had to be married for the job,' she said, and hoped against hope that that had a grain of truth in it, too. 'So he jilted me and, I imagine, looked around for someone else.'

'H'm. Oh, well, that has such a ring of truth about it that I don't think I will pursue it after all,' he said, half to himself. 'You told my mother all this, of course. What did she say?'

Ann's eyes widened. 'Indeed I did not, sir. She didn't even mention the matter of someone jilting me! I never for a moment suspected that anyone would,' she couldn't resist adding coldly.

He apparently didn't notice that last remark of hers. 'Why didn't my mother ask you that? Just what did you both discuss?'

'Opal, and my job here,' Ann said, with patience.

'Well, look, do sit down, there's a good girl. Fine, now I can relax in an easy chair even if I may not yet have my evening meal. Well, the thing is, I'm a busy man, and things being as they are, I imagine you will be as willing and ready as I am to get this over and done with in as short a time as possible.'

Thinking he meant this tiresome discussion, she said, 'I would indeed, sir.'

'*Howard,*' he reminded her, with such apparent feeling that she was moved to take him up on that point.

'I am going to be happy here, sir, I think, because I like Opal. I also believe I shall find I can like that poor soul who works here, Jago. I get on well enough with Mrs Farraker, too, and it is a part of the country I don't know and would like to know better. But, sir, with request, I do not feel that I can possibly go so far as to use your Christian name. If I seem too formal I could manage "Mr Crayne", for instance, but nothing else.'

'Why not? I know it's just a business arrangement, but if I'm to take my meals with someone perpetually calling me Mr Crayne, I shall not be at all easy. In fact, it will have a very bad effect on my temper!'

'Then don't take your meals with me, sir. I was aiming to take them with Opal. She expects it, anyway.'

With weary patience he raised his eyes to the ceiling. 'Then Opal shall take her meals with us too. Oh, hang it all, did not my mother warn you of this?'

'Indeed she didn't,' Ann said firmly, with that in her tone which suggested that she wouldn't have been there on his return if his mother had mentioned any such unattractive rule as that of taking her meals with the boss.

'I get the feeling that we are talking at cross purposes,' he said, after a thoughtful pause. 'I must dot the i's and cross the t's, I suppose, but if it is not necessary, you will forgive me, for in that case I fear you are being rather obtuse.' He drew a deep breath and said clearly, 'I expect my wife to take meals with me.'

Ann stared at him. 'But what has that to do with me, sir?'

'Oh, good grief, girl! Are you being funny, or don't you really know what this job is all about? You must know! It isn't a custom I know of to insist that an applicant for a job to look after a child had to be jilted!'

'Well, I did think it a bit odd at the time,' Ann admitted worriedly. 'But so much else claimed my attention in the advertisement that needed careful answering and thinking about, as it was after all, a resident job–'

'There is a very good reason why I must be married, and it concerns Opal,' he said slowly, his eyes never leaving hers. 'Believe me, I do not want a wife. Therefore, it struck me that a marriage of convenience would fit the bill, and for such a strictly business arrangement only a girl who had been jilted would consider such a thing. Do you agree with me on that point?'

She looked at him in utter bewilderment. It was the last thing she had imagined to have been suggested to her.

He mistook her expression and said with a trace of impatience, 'Good gracious, girl, it is all perfectly above board, I assure you – arranged properly with my solicitor. Knowing a bishop there has been no trouble where the licence is concerned – surely you as well as I would like to get this over quickly and quietly, and dispense with the curious outmoded custom of a honeymoon – even for appearance's sake? It is a kind of a job, for a definite and important purpose concerning Opal alone. But a job that would be worth your while financially – if you can bring yourself to be lucid enough to tell me if the sum I have arranged for your personal use in this capacity is enough for you?' And he mentioned what was really quite a generous figure.

But all Ann could think of was the first part of what he had said. 'Married? To you? For Opal's sake? But why? How would such a thing be for *her* sake?'

He looked as if he were going to explode, then altered his mind, saying, 'Well, yes, I concede, that is a fair question. Let us put it this way. I have a very good and explicit reason for having Opal brought up at home here and not sent away to school with other girls. An ordinary wedding would produce a wife who could argue round that point and be a great nuisance. But–'

'But a wife in name only, the business arrangement sort of wife, would have to do as she was told? I see,' Ann said quietly, but she seemed to slump a little in her seat, and suddenly she looked ineffably weary. Why – she asked herself – hadn't his mother mentioned it? Prepared her for this? And why should such a handsome man not have been married already? To say nothing of the reason he gave – a weird enough reason in all conscience when to romp with other girls would do Opal all the good in the world. A reason to be deeply suspicious of.

On the other hand, Ann swiftly and bleakly thought, what alternative had she? Perhaps a job in London, perhaps some sort of digs, undoubtedly more expensive than she could afford, as things were… A chilly prospect.

'You are not hesitating because of this Tom Westbury possibly changing his mind, are you?' Howard Crayne asked sharply. But to that question Ann could answer with swift and complete truth, 'No, indeed not!'

For perhaps the first time he looked satisfied. He stood up and pulled her to her feet. 'Don't shrink away from me,' he said, concisely, as if speaking to a child who expects a blow. 'Remember this is a job, and I want you to do it to the best of your ability. If you are short of money, then say so. Don't brood about it in silence. I can't stand people being silent and resentful. If there's anything you want to complain about, just come and tell me. Meantime, look after Opal.'

'That,' Ann said, with dignity, 'is the one thing I shall enjoy about the job. I like Opal very much. We get on well together.'

He looked a little surprised at that, but merely said, 'Good!' rather as if he didn't know quite what else to say. Privately he considered Opal a most tiresome child and something of a burden, which wasn't so surprising as he knew who Opal's parents were, and the whole circumstances of the case. But he was never one to look a gift horse in the mouth. If this quiet dignified girl was consenting to be his wife and to take the burden of Opal off his shoulders, who was he to question her tastes? Perhaps it was true that they did get on well together, for the moment, but even that was a godsend.

So he removed his hands from her shrinking shoulders, thrust them into his pockets, and said, 'Well, so that's settled! It is, isn't it? You're sure? No going back on the bargain, until I can get the wedding laid on!' and he said it as if the wedding was some tiresome business appointment looming ahead, the sort of thing that must be attended to but which would inevitably interfere with other things he would have much preferred to do.

'No, I'm quite sure,' Ann forced herself to say firmly. She would have liked more time to think it over, but then, to what purpose? It was marriage with this man or out on the labour market again. Severely scolding herself for being a fool, a chicken-hearted fool, wanting this cosy berth instead of braving the hazards of London and job-hunting, she looked up at him. And in his eyes she saw something that made her pause, consider her own position; was she so chicken-hearted? This was a job that she could well do, which two others had failed at. Opal needed her. And somehow, curiously, and in a way she didn't quite understand at this moment, but which was purely instinctive, she felt that this big handsome arrogant man needed her, too, even if at the moment he wasn't aware of it himself.

'Well, then,' he said briskly, 'don't worry about anything else, oh, except clothes. Good heavens, yes, you'll need new things. Speak to my mother about it. Yes, there had better be an account opened for you somewhere. Get someone to advise you about what you'll need, as my wife.' He flushed a little as he said it, and almost as if to cover his embarrassment, he said, 'Oh, lord, yes, I almost forgot – the ring. It's here some-where. It's an heirloom, so for goodness' sake don't lose it.' He brought out a small velvet box from his pocket, and got out a ring that even Ann, who had little knowledge of precious stones and fine settings, knew to be an important piece of jewellery. He swiftly picked up her left hand and slid the ring on her finger with a lift of the eyebrows because it was almost a perfect fit. 'Good heavens, that looks like a good omen, don't you think?' and he smiled at her, a smile that left her curiously shaken and feeling that she wished he would be serious, arrogant, impatient, anything, but not smile that smile of utter sweetness. She felt it should have been for someone else, not for her. 'Look, what am I thinking of?' he demanded. 'We're engaged. The ring fits. For heaven's sake let's go the whole way and go and see my mother, and then we'll tell Opal. After that, no need to do another thing. You'll find it will be all over the house and the district in no time.'

'Is it … going to be announced in the press?' Ann whispered.

'Have to be,' he said, striding by her side to the door. 'Must do it the proper way. Nothing hole and corner.'

'My clothes – have you any idea how much they are going to cost, to go with a ring like this?' she asked painfully.

He looked startled, then he smiled again. 'I knew I wasn't making a mistake!' he said, rather obscurely, she thought, and then nodding, he took her along to his mother's room, where they were reluctantly admitted, and rather frostily received. His mother listened to his announcement, then said coldly, 'If you've decided that's what you will do, my son, who am I to say anything against it?' and she distantly inclined her head to Ann, which was, Ann felt, the most horrible way to be congratulated on a forthcoming marriage. But then, of course, it was to be a marriage of convenience. A thing which would have to be explained to Opal, she supposed.

Opal had had her supper, and there had been tears, it appeared. Mrs Farraker was standing over her, waiting for the finishing of a supper that Opal was making a business of getting down.

'What's the matter?' Ann asked, looking from one to the other.

Opal hunched herself down further over the food she didn't want. Mrs Farraker said, 'I suppose you will be wanting to see to the child's eating yourself now, miss … madam, I should say.'

'What's that supposed to mean, Mrs Farraker?'

The housekeeper sniffed, and Opal said snuffling, 'They say you're going to marry

68

my Uncle Howard, and you might have told me first. Thought we were friends!'

'Who told you that?' Ann gasped, looking at the housekeeper.

Mrs Farraker said, staring at a point in the middle distance, 'Nobody knows how things get around in this house, miss. I should like to know myself.'

'How *did* you come by this information?' Ann persisted, feeling that here was something she must get to the bottom of at once.

'The girl from Bixley's farm, who isn't very bright, said she heard it in the air, all around everywhere,' Mrs Farraker said, as if she didn't like the explanation, but it was all she could say.

'What rot! She must have been listening at keyholes,' Ann said crossly. 'Do we really need her? It isn't nice to feel that nothing personal can be discussed without–'

'Old Mrs Crayne,' the housekeeper broke in, 'once gave a promise that the girl should be allowed to work here. It's all she can do. She isn't very bright. I don't know the circumstances but I do know that she won't be sacked.'

'Are you going to marry my Uncle Howard?' Opal insisted.

'Yes, pet,' Ann said quietly. 'Will you hate that very much?'

Opal said, 'I'd love it but you can't. He's married already!'

FOUR

Ann caught her breath, expecting the house-keeper to jump on the child as usual and be very irate with Opal for her outrageous stories. But for once the housekeeper was silent, flustered.

Ann showed the child her ring. 'I can assure you that whatever you've heard, Opal, it simply isn't true and I can prove it. Your uncle has told me that it's all been arranged with his solicitor, and a bishop so you see, it's absolutely all right. It must be, if people like that are in it.' And her serious tone stopped Opal's tears and made Mrs Farraker open her eyes wider and appear to be prepared to believe that.

'Well, I'm glad to hear it, madam, I must say, because there are some who will spread the most wicked rumours and I don't mind telling you there are a lot of wicked rumours flying about right now, and that's one of them.'

After the housekeeper had gone, presumably to put about what she had just heard (as Howard Crayne had rightly guessed she would) Ann sat down by the side of Opal. 'I haven't had any supper. What's that taste like?' and she matily picked up a clean fork and took a morsel off Opal's plate to try. 'Um, it's not bad. If you don't want it, I'll polish it off,' Ann said.

'There's some for you, under the covered dish there,' Opal said, 'and if you're going to eat yours then I'll eat mine. And ... and I'm awfully glad you're going to be my aunt because ... I like you!' she finished with a pathetic little rush.

'I'm glad because it wouldn't be up to much if you didn't,' Ann said, with a funny pucker of her lips which made Opal laugh. 'But let's make a pact, here and now, shall we? No more weird stories, eh? It's so uncomfortable for me because I don't know the people or the circumstances and you do. You know if it's true or not, so you ... have the advantage of me.'

'Is that good?' Opal wanted to know, liking the grown-up phrase.

'Good for you, but bad for me,' Ann said.

'I like the way you talk to me. Nobody else ever did.'

'Then you're lucky. Not many people get what they like. Mind you keep it, by being sensible,' Ann said. 'I tell you what – would you help me?'

Opal nodded vigorously. 'Can I do a handstand or two, to show you how happy I am?'

'Not just at the moment. Your supper wouldn't like it. Listen, I've got to buy a lot of new clothes, on account of being your uncle's wife. I can't go around in an old skirt and jersey any more, which is a pity but it can't be helped.' She looked at the child. 'I'd like someone to come with me and help me choose. Who would you suggest?'

'Not old Mrs Crayne,' Opal said at once.

'No, I think you've got something there,' Ann agreed. 'And the vicar's wife would hardly do.'

'Ugh, no, she's much too old-fashioned.' Opal toyed with her last bit of pudding. 'Promise you won't bite my head off if I say what I'm thinking?'

'What a thing to make me promise! All right, fire away!'

Opal screwed up her courage. 'Who do we know who's so posh?'

'Only old Mrs Crayne,' Ann frowned, holding on to her promise with difficulty, but the child was making a point and it wasn't far off the mark.

'That's what I mean. She's got an account with a great big shop in Leeds. No, not London, or Paris. She says it takes a small city to work really hard on a big order and they do you proud. Well, why don't you–'

'You're not going to suggest that I put my goods on Mrs Crayne's account from her shop?' Ann said, keeping her temper down with difficulty.

Opal gasped. 'I haven't finished. I was

going to say, why don't you ask Gertrude to go with you and choose, on her half day. She knows what's what and she's a good old scout. I think she likes you. Well, she didn't purse up her mouth all prissy at you when she passed you the other day, not like she used to at the others in this job.'

'But she's Mrs Crayne's maid and companion. She's in the enemy camp!' Ann protested.

Opal shook her head. 'Nope. Not the way I heard it. She told Mrs Farraker she thought you were a right nice young lady and Mrs Farraker almost agreed.'

'Did she now? And how, may I ask, did you hear that? Listening at keyholes?' Ann asked wrathfully.

A slow tear coursed its way down Opal's cheek. 'This isn't going to work, is it, you being Uncle Howard's wife. You're different already and I did like you so much. I did need you,' she said, and the last few words were only a muffled whisper.

'Then don't tell such whoppers, Opal!' Ann remonstrated.

'Not whoppers,' Opal said. 'I just heard it, like poor Zoë did.'

'All in the air, like voices!' Ann said heatedly. 'It won't do, Opal. You're spoiling everything.'

Opal considered her, then got up and leaned clumsily against her. 'I'm not, honest! It's peculiar, and it only happens where there's all the posh rooms. The whispers, I mean, where you hear things.'

Ann pulled herself together. 'You mean it's a sort of echo, like the sound carrying through a ventilating shaft? Then good heavens, child, who is listening to all these things we're discussing now and hoping, goodness knows, to keep them private and personal?'

Opal looked pleased and triumphant and faintly scared. 'That's what I'm trying to tell you! It doesn't happen up here. I don't know why. But I know it. That's why I kicked up such a rumpus and got banished to this part of the house.'

Ann let it go. She would hear nothing else that she could rely on, from Opal. She needed to have a good long talk with someone, about so many things. But who? Certainly not the housekeeper, whose allegiance was with anyone who would further her own cause – that of keeping her job and a place for that tragic son of hers. Not any of the other staff. Ann perceived that while labour conditions almost everywhere else were such that staff didn't hold to one place for long, confident that they could get work elsewhere if they grew tired, in this corner of England they had nothing else that was so easy, so useful to them; well-paid in the sense that they got their food and were near enough to home to be able to walk. No fares, no transport difficulties, a nice part of the country, and the ever-exciting day before them in a house that was reputed to be ... what? Haunted? Ann faced the fact and decided that it was either haunted or that Opal was even more steeped in her own fantasies than Ann had realised.

With these worries in her mind she abandoned the talk with Opal, but the child's appearance worried her. At that age, one needed to look nice to get confidence in one's self. Perhaps if Opal could be made to look nice and to enjoy it, she might stop being such a little exhibitionist.

'What was your hair like before you chopped it off?' she asked Opal.

'Long. Stringy.' Opal couldn't have been less brief or unhappy.

'I was wondering... There is a thing called an Urchin Cut, very cheeky but if it's done by a good hairdresser it looks proper. You know, the bits won't all stick out. Just like a boy's, it would be, and yet it would look proper, if you see what I mean. How about it?'

'How about what?' Opal said suspiciously.

'A trip to the big shops. Hairdresser's, outfitters – well, you'd like some pretty dresses, I suppose, to go with your new hair style. Well, for goodness' sake, Opal, I am going to be married and if I'm going to have new things, why shouldn't you?'

Opal perversely took that the wrong way. 'Oh, I see! I have to be at your wedding and you'd be ashamed of me if you didn't doll me up.'

Ann sighed in near exasperation. She dropped to her knees and held the child's shoulders. 'Darling, can't you believe that somehow, in the little time I've been here, I've come to like you very much?' she asked softly. 'And it did just occur to me that there really wasn't any need for you to look as if you'd chopped off your own hair–'

'But I did!'

'I know, but we don't necessarily have to leave it like that, do we, if we can make it look nicer? And you don't have to wear those things you have on, on Sunday, do you, if I can find you something really pretty and fashionable?'

'It wouldn't suit me,' Opal said flatly.

'How do you know till you've tried some things on? I tell you what–' She broke off and stared at Opal's round lens. 'When did you have those glasses?'

'Oh, I dunno. Ages ago. Can't see much without them.' Opal was supremely indifferent to her appearance, it was plain to see.

'Who was your optician? Someone in Oldbridge?' Ann persevered.

'No, Birmingham. Where I lived.'

'You lived in Birmingham? When was this?'

'Oh, about half a year ago. With a woman.'

'*Opal*,' Ann said warningly. She really wasn't in the mood for any more fantastic stories at that moment.

'It's true,' Opal said frantically. 'Honest, didn't you know? I haven't been here long. Only long enough to have two other people try out your job. I used to be just with anyone.'

'But,' Ann said, sitting back on her heels, 'I thought you were living in the big house of the great-uncle who was responsible for you, and he died so you came here. Isn't that it?'

'It's a bit like it, except that I never went in his house, only the once because he wanted to see what I looked like. Just before he died. He sort of stared, as if he couldn't believe it, and then he shuddered and said to a man—'

'—what man?' Ann demanded, determined to get at the truth if she could.

Opal made the effort. 'He was a sort of manservant or secretary or something. He did everything the old uncle wanted. He had brought me in a taxi.'

'From Birmingham. Who was the person you had been living with then?'

'I don't know. She only had a little house and she didn't like me but she told her friend that the pay made it worth while. Before that, I was with someone in Kidderminster only she moved. She used to be a maid at the house of the old uncle. She knew the woman in Birmingham.'

'Is that all?'

'No. Before that, I was with someone in Manchester. I didn't like that. It was a little grey street and the other kids used to play on the railway line. No, it's true, it's true. Ask Uncle Howard! He was furious about it. But he said it was past and done with and we'd got to forget it and the old uncle was too old and ill to be bothered by such things and that's why I was in queer places. Only—'

'Yes, darling?' Ann said softly, remembering her own not very happy childhood.

'Well, I think I was in a sort of school place at first. Well, there were other kids, boys as well as girls, only the grown-ups weren't very nice to us and when visitors came, they looked us over and took just one of us away.' She looked at Ann with a shrewdness that sat ill on her young face. 'It sounds a bit like an orphanage and people coming to adopt children, doesn't it? Only when I told Mrs Farraker, she said what a lot of rot.'

'Did she?' Ann murmured. She pulled Opal to her and held her close, absently, and oddly Opal didn't struggle to get away. 'Well, let's forget about all that, and give them all a surprise, shall we? I think we can make you look very attractive. And anyway, as I've got to buy some new things too, you

78

might as well come along to the shops and see what you like, don't you think?'

Opal didn't protest, which was odd. She looked rather depressed, Ann thought. 'Where are you going to get the money?' she asked at last.

Ann was startled. 'It's called credit. You just keep getting the things you need, and putting them on the account, which gets sent in to your Uncle Howard.'

'Better tell him first then,' Opal said, with grown-up wisdom, or else she had heard someone else talking about it. 'He'll have to tell the people in the shop that it's all right, before they'll let you start an account.'

Ann looked fierce. This was going to be rather as she had feared at first. Begging for things. Well, it was part of the job, wasn't it, to be his wife and the 'mother' of his ward, so she would go about it in a businesslike way. 'I'll put it all on old Mrs Crayne's account, then,' she said, with a satisfaction that cheered Opal, who for some reason couldn't stop laughing. And as an anticlimax, Howard sent her a note telling her he'd opened a bank account for her in Oldbridge and opened various credit accounts.

That was the day on which Ann discovered that although she had been told never to go out alone it was not easy to persuade anyone to take her. But Burridge was persuaded at last that they wanted – she and the child – to be taken into the town where the big shops were so he sighed, insisted on giving the car a complete wash down and overhaul, and even gave the time at which they could hope to be ready. By that time the whole household knew about it, except (it seemed) Howard and his mother. Really, Ann thought, the workings of this house were truly terrifying. Mrs Farraker gave Ann a list of things she couldn't buy locally and asked if she'd drop the order into Hattons' (Burridge would know where that was) and collect them on the way back. Zoë wanted some special sticky stuff to set her hair (she had saved up for it, she said) for the next local dance. Ann, sorry for the girl, who might have been rather pretty but for that vacant air in her young face, agreed to go. By the time she was ready, Ann had quite a list of things and wondered when they'd get time for their own shopping.

As they were about to start, Gertrude came quietly up the stairs to their floor, an odd look on her face. 'Do you want some shopping done, too?' Ann asked pleasantly, rather pleased that such an important person on the staff should ask her to do something.

Gertrude shook her head, came right up to Ann, and whispered, 'I would like to go along with you both.'

To say that Ann was surprised was to exaggerate. She was staggered, not only by

80

the request, but by the total absence of Gertrude's rather haughty manner. 'Why, yes, of course,' Ann said weakly, 'though we're not going to the pictures or anything. As a matter of fact–' she paused, wondering how she could manage to keep this a surprise if Mrs Crayne's maid were coming with them.

'I was going to suggest it, miss – madam, I should say. I did think – wonder–'

Opal was getting very tired of all this. 'We'll never get started!' she said, tugging at Ann. 'What she means is, she wants to choose your clothes. You'd better let her! She's wizard at it. She knows everything – all about High Society. She used to work for a duchess, didn't you?'

Ann shot a nervous glance at the maid, who Mrs Farraker had said was extremely temperamental (tetchy and above-herself were the words she used) and needed careful handling. Yet here was Opal treating her like a buddy of her own age, and quite staggeringly the woman looked down at Opal with an almost kindly look laced by a twinkle of amusement. 'Thank you, child, though I could wish that your elders might give me equal praise.'

So Gertrude went with them, quietly, almost secretly, out the back way to the car. 'It's actually my half day,' she excused herself to Ann, 'and Mr Burridge sometimes kindly drives me into the town.' So Ann, intercepting a look between the driver and Gertrude, guessed that that was the real reason for the delay. She sighed, and wished it could have been explained without fuss. But of course, in this house, such a thing wouldn't have happened. They lived on drama and intrigue, it seemed.

After Ann had got over everyone else's errands, she felt she could give themselves the pleasure of their own shopping, and was surprised by the look of approval she received from Gertrude when she reluctantly disclosed that her purpose had really been towards glamorising Opal. She was very glad of Gertrude's help then. Gertrude knew a small hairdresser in a quiet street who was really interested in the child, amused at the self-chopping effort and who made a really good job of the new styling. Opal didn't protest, oddly enough. Perhaps because the man who did the styling told her about his small sister's exploits, which intrigued Opal and worried Ann.

The optician was outside the town; they left Opal there for an eye test while Gertrude took Ann back to the big shops to help her choose things for herself.

Gertrude gave her a long and thoughtful look while things were being bought. 'Off the peg,' she murmured, with a sigh, as though it couldn't be helped. Time was so short. But in her mind's eye she was seeing Minerva, in those clever clothes made to suit her personality, with colour combinations that could never be found in this town. Well, Gertrude thought, bracing herself, this girl had something that Minerva hadn't, so if they couldn't match her personality in a hurry in Oldbridge, at least they could find clothes that would be a perfect foil for Minerva's flamboyance.

This girl, Gertrude saw with sudden pleasure, was like a quiet still lake, while Minerva was the thundering sea with stormy lights on it, or the blazing oranges and golds of a violent sunset. Ashamed of her own flights of fancy for the moment, she got down to the business of restraining the enthusiasm of the people in the shop, who could scent a large and perhaps continuing order, and found that Ann was quite agreeable to her choice. What Gertrude desired above all things was for Ann to wear something they could be sure Minerva wouldn't swamp by a near miss of colour, so for the first dinner party (which Gertrude knew about and Ann didn't) Ann was to wear, by Gertrude's clever choice, a dress so plain and well cut, exactly matching the quiet grey/blue of Ann's eyes. Gertrude also knew that to go with that magnificent engagement ring (which the shop people had of course noticed at once) there would be the Crayne Collar, an heirloom of five rows of fine matched pearls and a rather ornate pendant of pearls and emeralds. Gertrude smiled in anticipation of Minerva's anger at seeing the Crayne Collar on the slender neck of this quiet girl and for a moment the older woman was a little afraid. Never mind, she'd look after Ann, she suddenly decided, if only because she hated Minerva so much.

Ann was to dine with the family that evening. She knew that and had accepted it. Even Opal was to appear at dinner. It was a pity that the child's new and modern shaped glasses wouldn't be ready, but at the last moment Opal said to her, 'Are you sure I don't look soppy in this dress?' and when Ann had indignantly repudiated such an idea, Opal, with a brief glance down at new (and unscuffed) quite pretty shoes, stockings without a wrinkle or dirty mark on them, and hands manicured at the shop, she said, 'When we get down to the blue dining-room, Ann, can I put my hand on your arm? I want to surprise them and these glasses are a bit much. Thought I'd take them off.'

Ann said, 'It's a marvellous idea, pet, but we shall go into the green salon first for drinks, and I expect your Uncle Howard will expect me to go in on his arm. I suppose Gertrude will take his mother's arm–'

'No, Gertrude won't be down to dinner

tonight. Colonel Datchett with take Mrs Crayne. Dash, I forgot the drinks. How much can I see without these glasses?' and Opal snatched them off and experimented, delighted that she could do it without running into anything. Her small face puckered endearingly with a gamin grin. 'It's okay. I can manage by myself, at the last minute! How will I look?'

'Disturbingly attractive, I would say,' Ann frowned.

'Lumme. Isn't that good, then?'

'Yes, darling, very good. I was just surprised. You're going to be very attractive indeed when you grow up. We must work on it now, though. Let's give up some school lessons in favour of glamorising, shall we?'

'I say, I'm awfully glad you're the one who's going to marry my Uncle Howard,' Opal said impulsively, 'and not that other one!'

'Which other one?' Ann asked quickly, looking at the child's guilty face.

'Promise you won't be wild. I didn't mean to say that. If anyone says that Minerva was the one, don't take any notice.'

'Minerva– Who?' Ann asked carefully, her heart beating painfully.

'Mrs Thornton. The people in the kitchen say she's a rich widow but she was going to marry Uncle Howard once. And now she's come back. Don't listen to them.'

Old Mrs Crayne was not happy about the first dinner party at all. She had had to break what was becoming a hard and fast rule, and invite the heads of local society to dinner. That was necessary to introduce the fiancée of her son, but she considered that the Datchetts and the Quarleys were far beneath her. Sir Victor had started life as a boat-builder's son but had amassed a fortune with his new light-weight hulled yacht which he had built locally, thereby endearing himself to the county for providing employment in the old way. Mrs Quarley had brought her own fortune, won, Mrs Crayne often said, in supreme distaste, from gambling. Their son was an insipid produce of university, and refused to go into the family firm. But they had to come, and the worst of it was, they knew all about Howard's earlier life. But it couldn't be helped. Howard had for some reason changed his mind about being secretive about his marriage. Nothing hole-and-corner, he had suddenly decided. Well, for heaven's sake, what else was it?'

She was angry, fretted, and couldn't think of a single way to set that girl Ann down, before the dinner, until she remembered that they were at the last minute short-staffed. Ann could help set out the drinks in the drawing-room, she thought with satis-faction, and gave orders to that effect.

She wasn't aware of it, but the staff didn't

like it. They had seen Ann, dressed rather early, but not in any way nervous. Her pale hair, a honey gold, and slightly wavy had been swept up in a style Gertrude had copied from a magazine imported from Paris. It set off to perfection the Crayne Collar which she had been sent with. Tradition held that Mrs Crayne herself, in getting it out of the hidden safe in her room, should have presented it to her future daughter-in-law, but that was another thing she couldn't bring herself to do. Gertrude put it round Ann's neck, and could have cried to think that this lovely creature, who had somehow quietly blossomed into just what they all had dreamed of as the new chatelaine of Kingsbride, should have to help the maids.

Ann didn't mind. She looked into Gertrude's distressed face, smiled and touched her on the shoulder. 'Dear Gertrude, don't care so much! I feel you're going to be a real friend to me, and heaven knows, I do need one, but you must see this thing in its true perspective. You must all be well aware that this is all part of my job,' and her quick glance revealed acceptance of that, before Mrs Crayne's companion lowered her eyes. 'Well, then, it's a job with many facets, and one of them is to help out tonight as we're short-staffed. Gertrude, it isn't I who count – it's Opal. We must remember that. In a sense, it's her night.'

Gertrude blessed her for that, and promised to see that Opal didn't get messed up at the last minute, in a bad mood. The child was only being allowed to stay down for the meal, then she would be banished to bed, and she would miss Ann's goodnight kiss. Ann was about to ask Gertrude how she could manage to slip away unnoticed for that, when Gertrude remembered something. 'Miss – ma'am, I should say – there's something I should tell you. Mr Howard once had a terribly tragic love affair–'

She looked so upset and time was running short, so Ann thought she'd put her out of her misery and admit she'd heard something about Minerva and that she wasn't afraid, even though it appeared Minerva would be there tonight. 'I know about it – don't worry,' she said, and couldn't understand Gertrude's astonished glance. But the housekeeper appeared, calling her, so the moment was lost, and Gertrude had no other opportunity to say what she felt she must.

So Ann was totally unprepared for the way Howard received her that evening. She was settling out the last tray of glasses in their small embroidered drip mats, when he came into the green salon. It was a gloomy room, lit by branches of candles (his mother's idea) and Ann was standing in front of one. To him, as he stood horrified at the door, it wasn't Ann in the soft grey dress, with the Crayne Collar, and her hair piled high against the glowing candles. It was that other one...

FIVE

She looked up startled at a sound near the door and saw his face. 'What is it?' she asked, frowning. 'Oh, don't say you're going to be upset because I'm helping with the drinks – it was your mother's idea so it's all right.'

That didn't improve matters. His white face took on a sullen brick red for a moment, and she realised then what bad feeling there was over this engagement of his. He closed the door behind him and walked slowly across the room towards her. 'What made you do your hair like that?'

'I thought it might be more festive, and go with this dress and ... the occasion. Don't you like it?'

'Go and do it the way you usually do,' he said curtly. 'And don't be long. What did my mother say when she put the collar round your neck?'

'Gertrude did it, in my room,' she said, puzzled, and saw too late that that was merely adding more fuel to the fire.

He looked very frustrated. He stood there for a moment, looking at her. He stood silent for so long, she put down the glasses she held and said, 'Look, what's the matter?

Haven't I got suitable things on? Is it the colour? I am really trying to do the best I can in this job–'

He turned away, with a movement of his hands and shoulders that suggested to her utter defeat. 'Oh, never mind,' he said. 'Leave those glasses and run up and do your hair again. It's for your own good. I don't think you'll like the guests to say that it reminds them of someone else, I'm sure.'

Ann's face cleared. 'Oh, so that's it! Well, I don't mind!' Minerva, no doubt. She was looking forward to seeing this rich widow who seemed to have such an influence in this place, even though apparently she threw Howard over for a rich man.

'Well, I do mind!' he snapped. 'And please give me the same sort of obedience that you would to any other employer.' It was out. He hadn't intended that thought to escape from his tired brain. He was all contrite. 'I really am sorry. I shouldn't have said that! I didn't mean to!'

'But it *is* said,' Ann said quietly. 'Words are like deeds, they cannot be undone. I don't know who said that first, but it's very true.'

'Well, if you must know, this is a precision job, just like something on the drawing-board. It's no use looking surprised. The reason is private and personal and to be honest, I sensed a certain amount of tugging the other way on your part so I had to nip it

91

in the bud. Believe me, this marriage, even though it is just a job for you, is really of the utmost importance to me. Nothing must get in its way.'

'Could something?' she asked levelly. 'If so, don't you think you should tell me what it is, to put me on my guard, or how shall I recognise it when it comes?'

'Just do as I say, and you'll do fine,' he said evasively, but as she still stood there, he seemed to waver a little. Something about her upset him. It hadn't been there quite so much before, not since the moment he had seen her in the hollow on the moor, struggling with Jago and the child to keep a tight hold on the injured bird. He hadn't recognised it for what it was then. He had been so surprised at the set-up. Now he saw that although this girl looked quiet and tractable on the surface, she wasn't really. Like Gertrude, he sensed that she would obstruct him in many ways, if she felt like it, or believed that what she was doing was right. She was no quiet person to do as she was told to the last degree.

She held his glance for a long time, then suddenly, for reasons of her own, she looked away, shrugged a little, and walked past him. 'I'll rearrange my hair,' she said, and there was that in her tone that made him sorry he had insisted. But he couldn't help it. Someone (who, for heaven's sake?) had done her hair that way purposely, to rake up old memories. But who?

Ann was worried about that, too. She tried to find Gertrude to ask her about it, but there was trouble about Opal.

Ann forgot that she must alter her hair. Opal was crying piteously, the housekeeper standing over her. 'Look at what you've done to your new dress! What Mrs Crayne will say, I don't know!'

'I don't care!' Opal howled, and then she became aware that Ann was in the room. She stopped her wild crying with difficulty, and when it was controlled to hiccupping sniffs, Ann asked quietly, 'What happened, my dear?'

Opal said in a surly voice. 'It was *her!* She laughed at me. Said I looked silly. And then she put out her foot and tripped me.'

'Oh, Opal, Mrs Farraker would never–' but the housekeeper cut it swiftly. 'She means Mrs Thornton, miss. And why that child was anywhere near the guests, I can't think!'

'It was that Minerva! She did it purposely,' Opal insisted. 'Just to make them all see I'd left off my glasses and couldn't do without them and I looked good and silly and I won't try that again!'

'I can't believe that one of the guests would do such a thing,' Ann repeated, but there it was. 'What is it, spilt all down your dress, that pretty new dress?' Ann was as upset as Opal.

'It was her drink. You'd just gone out of that room and Uncle Howard was there and I thought I'd try out on him how I could get about without glasses only *she* must have gone in by the other door and they were talking and she *spoilt* it all! And why did he have to pour out a *red* drink for her? It looks like blood,' Opal added ghoulishly with a glance at the housekeeper.

Mrs Farraker sniffed angrily. 'I expect she got in Mrs Thornton's way, miss, that's about the fact of the matter. And it's no use shouting at me, Opal – because I know you! I know all about your tricks!' she said to Opal.

When they were alone, Ann tried to persuade Opal to change into the other nice dress that had been bought for her, but Opal had gone off the idea altogether. 'Besides, they'll tell Mrs Crayne and she won't want me down there to dinner. Besides, it'll be pretty boring. That Mrs Thornton is the sort of person who looks at you and all the gentlemen think she's smiling nicely but you know inside you that she's having a jolly good laugh at you. I'm not having that. I don't *have* to go down to dinner!'

'But you will eat what's sent up here for you, won't you, pet?'

'Honestly, I can't understand you, Ann! I thought you'd be livid, like ole Farraker!

Well, you know what I mean. Why are you so nice to me?'

'It just might be because I have discovered getting livid and steamed up makes me tired,' Ann said, which made Opal giggle. She looked thoughtfully at the child as she changed her out of the spoilt dress. She would put it into soak, but it would never be the same again.

'Don't worry about this. It was just an accident, I'm sure. Well, let's pretend it was an accident. No sense in brooding over it. And I'll tell you all about the dinner party when I come up, shall I?'

Opal nodded and rushed at Ann and hugged her, which didn't help her new dress and the hairstyle much, but there wasn't time to do anything about either now. She looked at Opal and wondered if she could trust the child, to ask her about the people downstairs. Opal would know them, she supposed, in that uncanny way the child had, although she apparently hadn't been here long. But somehow, something about pumping the child for that information didn't appeal to her. She kissed Opal, and said she'd be back as soon as she could. Then she went downstairs, weighed down by the Crayne Collar, uncomfortably aware that she hadn't had time to change a hairstyle that surely Gertrude should have known was an unwise choice, and not at all sure of

Howard's reception of her.

Howard was on his way to find her. She and he met at the top of the grand staircase and his glance flew to her hair. She said, 'I'm sorry, but what with one thing and another, there wasn't time to do anything about it. I did mean to!'

'Go and do something about it now. I'll come with you and wait outside the door, in case you forget something else.'

She grinned at him and a fleeting smile touched his severe mouth. 'What happened about poor little Opal?' she asked him.

'Oh, that child is in trouble wherever she is. I can't think what mischief prompted her to leave her glasses behind, but she stumbled, as she should have known very well that she would! Never mind the damage to her clothes, what about the carpet?'

'How much was spilt on the carpet?' Ann asked faintly, remembering that luxurious article and of how she had almost been afraid to tread on it.

'A tiny spot, Thank heavens little other damage was done before we got that child on her way upstairs again!'

Ann's breath was released sharply with relief, then she thought of Opal. 'Poor scrap, she discovered she could walk carefully without her glasses. I think her sight must be improving – the old glasses were too strong. And she did so much want to surprise you, to see her in her new clothes and without those awful specs. Poor Opal! Everything goes wrong for her!'

'You sound as if you like her!' Surprise cut through his tones.

'Well, of course I do. She's not half bad underneath. A delightful urchin, but she's so lonely and she knows people don't like her. She wants to be loved, and that, surely, isn't an unreasonable thing to want. You don't have to pay for love!'

'My dear, the words of wisdom that keep on falling from your young lips,' and then they had reached the door of her room.

Stung by what seemed to be sarcasm from him, her glance winged to his face, but there was only ineffable tenderness and sadness there. 'If you don't believe me,' he continued, 'when I assure you that love is not the free commodity you think it is, then I don't quite know what I shall do with you.'

'Of course love's free!' she insisted.

'No,' he said definitely, the smile and the tenderness now gone, leaving only a harsh look that seemed to spring from some memory. 'Love has to be paid for, to the last farthing, believe me. If you're lucky, you can earn it, by sheer effort; if you're not lucky, then you have to pay, in cold cash, or kind. There's always a bargain angle to it.'

'How bitter you are!' she said, wonderingly.

'I'm surprised that you aren't bitter!' he retorted, thereby reminding her that she was supposed to have been jilted.

She flushed a little and looked down at her hands, thinking of Felicity and the way she had shamelessly taken away from Ann, time and time again, either some nice man who might possibly have wanted to talk to Ann, or the opportunity to meet any of them on even ground. Felicity had to take, whether she wanted the person or not. Ann said quietly, 'I suppose I ought to be bitter,' but she found she couldn't be bitter about Felicity's greed and conniving ways. What was the use? Besides, there was always the hope that now she had got away from Felicity, she would meet someone and not have things so arranged that there was nothing in it for her. Bitter? 'No, I'm not really bitter,' she murmured, and turned and went into her room.

The matter of her appearance was a problem. Without Gertrude's excellent help and taste, what could she do with her hair but tie it back with a ribbon as usual? She went to the door, one arm raised to her head, her hand holding back her long hair in a casual figure of eight. 'How this?' and she swung round for him to see the view of the back.

'Why can't you do it the way you do every day?' he asked in genuine bewilderment, so she said dispiritedly, thinking of how the effect of the dress and the collar would be lost without the elaborate hairstyle, 'All right. Won't be a minute,' and she shut the door on him. They weren't married yet and when they were, it would make no difference, she told herself with a little scared flutter. Why, she asked herself, as she finally compromised and tied her long hair in a hanging coil behind her neck, with a soft blue-grey velvet ribbon, why did he shatter her so, with all this talk of marriage? As he had insisted, it was just a job. Everybody, even the staff, knew that!

Finally she went out to him and stood for his approbation, bringing a very startled look to his face. For now, with the dress and the Crayne Collar, and that half-simple half-sophisticated coil and ribbon bow, she had a young appeal that was stunning. What would Minerva say, he wondered, or *do?* All of a sudden he was afraid for Ann, and what he was planning for her future.

He said curtly, 'It will have to. We're very late now,' and they went down together.

But in the event, Minerva was not nasty to Ann. And nobody expressed any surprise at Ann's appearance because she no longer looked like someone Howard had ever known. They were all very nice to her and Mrs Crayne, for reasons of her own, set out to be gracious, if not actually friendly.

Minerva took Ann's breath away. As Gertrude could have told her, Minerva was one of those women who gave the illusion of great beauty, by means of dramatising themselves successfully. Minerva was like the sun, and the rest of the people in the room seemed to Ann to be merely tiresome shadows, spoiling the main thing she wanted to look at. Minerva now had such bright tones to her yellow hair, that even to Ann it looked artificial, yet it suited Minerva so much. And the whole of her personality swamped everyone else's so that only Howard and his mother bothered to say anything much. You couldn't put Mrs Crayne into the background, and Howard's personality was, as Ann had discovered swamping in its own way. They and Minerva held the stage, leaving Ann, the Datchett couple and the Quarley family very much in the background. Minerva's way of keeping herself in the foreground of someone else's engagement party, Ann later discovered, after it was all over and she had gone to her room, was to go out of her way to be nice to Ann, and to reminisce with Howard, so that Ann should know all about the things he liked doing and the things he had done. Minerva made a great success of it. Ann was sure that everybody would go home remembering what Minerva had said and done, and not even be able to call up a picture of Ann in their minds. But then, Ann thought, with a rueful half smile at herself in the mirror as she listened to Gertrude's quick footsteps pattering along the corridor, coming to take the Crayne Collar off that slender young throat, wasn't it always the same? Ann never did hold the stage. People rarely remembered what she had been wearing or even what she looked like. She half smiled and turned to Gertrude, and then she remembered something.

'Look at my hair! Mr Crayne made me take down that lovely upsweep you did. He said it would be uncomfortable – people would remember someone else who had it. He was very cross. Why did you do it?'

Gertrude looked taken aback at that speech. 'But I tried to tell you why I did it, dear. I didn't want you to be swamped by Mrs Thornton. She has that effect on people.'

It seemed incomprehensible to Ann that a hairstyle belonging to a person should be considered necessary to someone else in order that they shouldn't be swamped by that same person. She framed a question, but never uttered it. Why bother? Gertrude had undoubtedly meant well and was probably quite surprised to think that Howard Crayne had taken umbrage. How he must make the lives of the staff uncomfortable, with his unpredictable ways, Ann thought!

The following day set in really fine and warm, so Ann thought she would take Opal out in the fresh air and try to wash away the taste of yesterday's unfortunate stretch of hours. 'You need a pet of your own,' she frowned.

Opal had a trick of watching warily, with indrawn breath, when she expected something nice to happen. Ann went on, 'I wonder if Mrs Farraker could tell us where Jago got his dogs from?'

Opal was horrified. 'No, don't let her *know!* He's not supposed to have animals of his own.'

'Why not?' Ann paused in her stride over the tufty turf to consider the child and what new picture she had conjured up.

'Because if he goes mad he might hurt them,' Opal said.

There was a long silence during which the wind buffeted them, and brought with it the scent of seaweed and the mass of things growing on the cliff-tops. At last Ann said, 'I suppose you wouldn't like to take that back and try something else? Or perhaps I'd better forget all about the subject and we'll consider what we're going to do about next term's lessons, because,' she said fiercely, looking very hard down into the child's eyes, 'whatever else happens, I am going to make sure I get you educated.'

Opal hunched her shoulders. Clearly she wasn't going to say anything else about Jago so Ann concluded that it must have been something she had overheard in the kitchen.

That was another mystery Ann had to solve: how the child ever managed to hear what was going on down in the base of the manor.

'Some people might think,' Ann continued conversationally, as she struck off at the crossroads for the village of Regent's Bay without a word to Opal about what that might portend in the way of shopping, 'that education was a dreary old business of books and sums and dates of wars and deaths of kings...'

'That's from a poem,' Opal put in, in a surly voice, which made Ann catch her breath with sheer delight. Take Opal in your stride and you never knew what might come out of that sharp brain of hers.

But it didn't do to say such a thing out loud, of course. 'And yet recalls the very hour,' she encouraged, but Opal had let one thing slip that she hadn't meant to, and enough was enough. Ann recited the rest of the poem to her, remarking mid-way, 'And pausing here set down its load of pine-scents... That's my favourite line. I can't think of a better line about the wind, can you?'

Opal shrugged, so Ann asked, 'You don't happen to know who wrote that poem, I suppose?'

Opal said, 'Course not,' so Ann said mildly, 'Well, that's education, d'you see? You see a bit of poetry, you like it, you read it through once or twice and it sticks, then you remember the title, but you don't stop there. You look at the poet's name, and if you have time, you look him up in the encyclopaedia, and the chances are that he did other things besides writing poetry, like Herrick, who was a country parson and a very interesting person, and ... oh, well, I could go on and on. It's my favourite thing.'

No answer from Opal, so Ann tried again. 'Mind you, I adore dogs, and I have a book by Kipling which was supposed to have been written by a dog. It's a super book. And it has just occurred to me that in this very village is a house where a bright little black bitch has just had another littler. D'you suppose they'd let us take a look at them?'

Then at last Opal came up for air, as it were. Her face lit, then at once clouded. ''Course not. It's too soon.' So Ann said, 'Then how about us finding out when we could take a peep, and perhaps you wouldn't mind waiting while I get some ice cream – I know you aren't in the mood for any.'

Opal's astonishment was ludicrous. Ann couldn't help laughing. Opal joined in, and went a step further in her painful unbending; she took Ann's arm and hung on to it as she danced along. 'You're super! You're fun!' she chanted.

The place that sold ice cream was at the

end of the village, next door to the iron-monger's. They were just coming away with giant cornets in which were stuck bits of chocolate and jelly babies. Opal was enchanted and found a fine bit of shade in which to stand and lick hers, so that the sun wouldn't melt it. It was early in the year for ice cream to be sold. The shopkeeper made it herself, she told Ann, and looked curiously at the girl whose name was already linked with that of Howard Crayne, in the way things got out in this village. Suddenly Jago emerged from the ironmonger's with his purchases sticking out of the newspaper wrapped parcel. He saw Ann and stared, smiling ludicrously at her, just standing there.

Ann lifted her cornet. 'Want one?' she asked him and turned to the woman behind the counter.

'Oh, miss, I wouldn't...' the woman began, but Ann's eyebrows shot up, and they embraced Opal who had emerged like lightning from her shade to deliver the warning that the shopkeeper had forestalled her in.

Silenced, they both watched Ann purchase a cornet and gravely hold it out to Jago. He stared, his face fading. Doubt came in his face. He knew he shouldn't. 'Not my birthday,' he muttered, looking as if he were going to cry.

'Yes, birthday present,' Ann said firmly. 'I wasn't sure when you had your birthday. It's a late present.'

His face was one huge adoring smile. 'Late birthday present,' he echoed, then told the shopkeeper it was a late birthday present, and then told Opal. 'Put your parcel down on the ground,' Ann said firmly. 'Take the cornet and go over there in the shade and eat it. Then I want to talk to you. There's an errand you can do for me.'

'Errand, yes,' he said eagerly, and departed.

'He does just as you tell him, miss!' the shopkeeper marvelled.

'What's the matter with him?' Ann asked quietly, an eye on Opal. 'Just simple, I suspect? Harmless?'

The woman looked acutely uncomfortable.

'Go over there in your bit of shade, Opal,' Ann said kindly, smiling encouragingly at the child. 'I'll call you in a minute. Now,' she said, turning to the woman, 'I have no doubt that you are all aware that I am to be Mrs Howard Crayne soon,' and the woman's face was proof enough of that. 'All right, I know villages. I have nothing against the interest of everyone, provided it is just interest, and that I know about it. Now, what is the feeling of the village towards that poor soul?' and she quirked an eyebrow at Jago.

'Well, miss, we know all about him. He was born here. Maud Farraker's one of us.

But we don't know who his father was. Oh, he'll stay on at the manor so long as nothing bad happens. The Craynes, begging your pardon, miss, protect their own. You've got a way with you. I've never seen him like that to anyone he hadn't known all his life, and then not always. Only...'

'Yes?' Ann took her up with determination. 'I must know all about it.'

'Well, if something annoys him, he gets a bit nasty, if you see what I mean. Like for instance...'

'Like someone hurting one of his pets?' Ann guessed, and the woman's face lit with a warm smile. 'That's right, miss,' was all she said, however, and turned to another customer who was coming up.

Ann nodded to her, called Opal and they strolled back to the chemist. Jago was behind them, licking his cornet ecstatically. 'Wait outside, please, Jago. Won't be long,' she said, and they went inside to buy a special shampoo for Opal, and some simple manicure things she had never had before. Ann topped up her supply of tissues, and asked Opal's advice about the smell of some toilet water and hand cream, which filled the child with importance and pride. Then they went outside and picked Jago up.

'Dogs, Jago,' Ann started, having discovered early on in their acquaintance that if one introduced a subject with one word, he caught on quickly; several words all at once and he was lost and frightened.

'Dogs, yes,' he said, pleased and excited.

'Ann,' Opal warned, tugging her sleeve.

'Where could I find a puppy, Jago? For me to keep,' she added.

'Ann, don't,' Opal pleaded, but Jago was off and away. He kept up a half-stooping, half-lolloping trot that covered the ground quickly and didn't tire him. 'It's all right,' Ann said. 'He'll take us to see the new litter. I'm not sure which house it is.'

'He won't,' Opal moaned. She knew where he was going.

Ann saw the wisdom of listening to the child's warnings, when they arrived at the back of the village, where the houses were poor, ill-kept, with thin grubby children playing in a stream that ran along where normally the kerb would be. One little boy had a paper boat he had made with a matchbox and a label for a sail. It kept sinking. None of the children laughed. A bigger boy was making them nervous. Presently he emerged from a doorway with a wretched puppy and two cans tied to its tail. He prodded it with a stick.

Opal wailed, 'Don't let Jago–' But it was too late. With a roar, Jago rushed at the boy. 'I told you so!' Opal sobbed.

Ann's clear voice cut through the noise. 'Jago, pick up the puppy for me, will you?

Never mind the boy.' She repeated, 'Pick up the puppy.'

As if mesmerised, he quietened, tenderly picked up the little animal and brought it back to Ann, nothing left of the big boy but his thundering footsteps round the corner of the poor little street. Ann said, 'Let's take the cans off his tail, and then we'll find some food for him. Now where?'

Opal and Jago stared at each other. Opal looked despairing. Ann said, 'What is it?' so Opal said, 'This is how he gets all those animals who follow him and his mother doesn't know. There'll be such a row!'

'No! No trouble! It's her'n!' Jago said anxiously, trying to put the puppy in Ann's arms.

'Don't take it, Ann! It'll have insects in it,' Opal sobbed.

'Don't be silly, darling. Making such a fuss. Give it to me, Jago. Home now – bath?' and she indicated the little shivering animal. 'All we have to do,' she explained to Opal, 'is to put some disinfectant in the water. Then we'll give him some milky food.'

She noticed the crowd pressing against her. Children and women from the houses. Curious, their eyes on her engagement ring. Opal said, 'Let's go. I know I'm never fit to be seen, but I wouldn't come here, not for anything. They've got bad drains.'

Ann hushed her. Jago's size was protecting

them, she guessed. 'Jago, is there a little cat that wants a good home?' eliciting a further wail of horror from Opal.

'You can have this thieving little monster, if you want it,' a woman said, thrusting a dirty bit of tabby fur at her. 'For a price!'

Ann said indignantly, 'Certainly not! Think yourself lucky I am not going to bring an animal inspector here; tin cans' on puppies' tails and that poor scrap half starved!' and she threw up her head furiously. The little crowd fell back and made way for them, and the curious procession wended its way from the back of the village. Jago, it appeared, knew a short cut through a copse of thin trees. Opal was crying quietly, and the animals made unhappy noises, too. Not a very propitious day in the village, Ann thought.

Suddenly the funny side of it caught her and she started to laugh. Jago looked startled, and Opal promptly stopped crying. Ann said, 'Water, that's what we want, to clean us all up. We look terrible. And we're so near the sea. Let's!' and this time Opal merely looked terrified.

Jago thought it a terrific idea. He changed his tracks and led them down one of those narrow cuttings between the high rocks, that the county produces so suddenly and enchantingly. It was worthy of a camera, with the strong light of unseasonable sunshine.

Opal said, 'Ann, what's got into you? I can't bathe! Neither can you! We haven't got swimsuits and besides, I haven't got permission. But look at him! He's mad, I tell you!'

'I didn't say immerse in the water, silly, but we can duck the little dog, the cat too, and then I'll wrap the cat in my scarf on the way back and he'll be all right, and neither of them will be so bad to look at. As for us, we can wash our hands in good sea water, can't we?'

'But Jago thinks you mean *swim!* Look at him!'

Jago was like a child, jumping up and down on a rock. He had torn off his thick sweater and shoes, and stood in his tight shrunken trousers and without waiting for Ann's warning, he jumped from the rock in a perfect arc, entering the water smoothly, almost without a splash.

'What will the housekeeper say?' Opal whispered.

'For a little girl who gets into the scrapes that you do, you are behaving very oddly today,' Ann said severely. 'You watch Jago. I have never seen such fine diving in my life. Look at him swimming back! He's marvellous in the water!' Marvellously good-looking, too, she thought, now he had something serious to do, which wiped that silly grin off his face. But she knew better than to say so.

'Very good, Jago,' she said, as he came out. 'Give the puppy a ducking, will you, while I wash the kitten?' which gave him an important part in the proceedings. The puppy's struggles were helpless in his great hands, which were amazingly gentle. The kitten struggled, too, but all the while she rid it of its insect life, she chatted to Jago. 'How's the bird we made better?'

'Bird flying now,' he said, over and over, till Ann thought of something else to ask him. 'How will you get dry, Jago? Mustn't stay wet.'

'Run about,' he said. 'Like this!' and demonstrated.

'Oh dear, that poor puppy,' Ann said, smiling at the demonstration.

Opal was helping her with the kitten which was by now too frightened to do anything but crouch in the folds of Ann's scarf. Suddenly Opal screamed.

'What's the matter, darling?' Ann shot round to ask.

Jago returned, pelting over the sand, obviously thinking the kitten had scratched his idol. For an agonising moment they stared at him, terrified that he'd do the kitten a mischief. Opal, jumping up and down, cried, 'Your ring, Ann! You've lost it! It's a family heirloom!' and they all stared down in horror at her now bare fourth finger. The Crayne engagement ring had gone.

SIX

It was one of the most awful moments of Ann's life. One moment they had all been so happy; the next, by one small observation on Opal's part, they were shattered. And with good reason.

'Where could I have lost it?' Ann whispered. 'We'll have to go back to the village and search every step of the way.'

'But we went through the woods,' objected Opal. 'And we came down the gap. If you'd dropped it there, you'd never find it among all those small stones and shells.'

'And I've been washing the kitten in the water,' Ann said slowly. 'And it struggled, and scratched me, and I almost lost the poor little thing!'

'I could have told you that cats don't like water,' Opal ventured, curiously reluctant to be rude at this moment, for some reason best known to herself. Ann looked curiously at her, and decided that the child must be in a lonely mood and unwilling to upset Ann by anything she might do herself, and so lose her only protector.

Ann said briskly, 'Cats don't *like* getting wet, I know, but this kitten was in a bad

113

state. It was sea water or a bath with disinfectant, and I'm quite sure it wouldn't have liked that! Now don't stand shaking your head at me – have you never watched a cat picking its way through long wet grass when it was stalking a bird? They will get wet if it's something they need to do, so don't think the sky's fallen in because this little wretch is now clean.'

'He'll lick himself and get sea water on his tongue,' Opal sobbed.

'Better than getting disinfectant on it,' Ann retorted. 'What am I to do about that ring, though?'

Jago was hopping up and down. 'Where? I look, I go see, but where? Where?' Sometimes he was almost lucid, Ann thought distractedly.

'I suggest we all split up and search in different places,' was all she could think of. 'Jago, I was wearing a ring. Do you remember what it looked like? All sparkly and shiny?'

He nodded excitedly. 'Gold ring?' he said over and over again.

'I've lost it. We must find it. No, don't run away. Come back while I think where we should search.' At least it would keep him on the move and get him dry, she thought distractedly.

It was getting on: they should have been returning to Kingsbride. But they must

114

search first. So, holding the puppy and kitten tightly, they retraced their steps, Jago running to and fro, looking on the ground, until they reached the little copse. There her heart sank. If she had dropped it here, those children would have found it, and it was doubtful if anyone would have admitted it. She looked into the hostile faces of the woman still standing leaning on their front gates, gossiping, and the children, bowling hoops and setting out treasures of bits of stone and glass in rows in the gulley by the stream. 'Let's go back,' she said to Opal and Jago, as some children began to clamour that she was holding their cat.

'We've lost that ring,' Ann said, as the copse swallowed them up. 'And what I shall say to Mr Crayne, I can't think.'

'Why don't you call him Howard? He's going to be your husband!'

'Oh, Opal,' she sighed. 'I can't. He's still a stranger to me,' was the best she could offer by way of explanation. 'Look at Jago. If that ring is on the ground anywhere, he'll find it!'

Jago was still slowly jog-trotting, but from side to side, searching the surface of the ground, and as he was running with bare feet, he would surely have found it. In that way, they got through the gap and down to the water's edge. The sea was running out. Low tide wasn't yet, but it was near enough to make the surface of the water still, with hardly the lap of a small wave. She went and sat on a boulder and stared down into the depths of the quiet water. Jago, still holding the puppy and his newspaper parcel, was standing looking hard at her, waiting for the next instructions. Opal was staring at her miserably through her thick lens, her hair awry, her clothes crumpled and none too clean. Ann felt she couldn't meet their eyes any more. She didn't know what to say to them, to help them out of this disaster. She remembered the ring's worth, and Howard's face as he had mentioned it. She stared at the hard, rippled surface of the sea bed, and saw his face, cold and ruthless, consumed with fierce anger that she had wantonly lost a family heirloom, while out on this ridiculous errand with the child, two stray animals and a simpleton that Howard probably didn't even realise was such a part of his household. And as she stared, the gentle movement of the receding tide shifted a lump of seaweed off something on which it had been caught – something half submerged ... the engagement ring.

'It's there!' Her voice was raised, but croaky. The other two joined her, but to see into that depth of water they both had to crowd on the same ledge of rock on which she was crouched. That was how Howard saw her, as he quietly arrived on his great roan, Minerva riding beside him on a slightly smaller grey.

Opal said, 'How can we get it? It's too deep!' but Jago shouted, 'I get it! I get it!' and stood up and did one of his superb dives. The puppy crouched shivering beside Ann, whimpering, his owner lost. They were all too much interested in what was in the water to realise they were no longer alone. Howard looked at Ann's face, as she leaned over, waiting, for Jago to surface; clutching the kitten, shawl-wrapped, to her, the other arm around Opal and her hand also managing to keep a hold on the puppy. It was that unconsciously *embracing* attitude of hers, that had impressed him before. Whenever he saw her, she was either physically holding someone to her, or mentally caring for them, daring to speak up on their behalf.

He was about to call out to them when Minerva, her hand on his arm, said, 'That girl worries me! Not a very healthy friendship, is it, with that half-wit. Where does he come from?'

Howard's lips tightened. 'Everyone knows about Jago. He's all right!' but Minerva persisted. 'But for the child's sake! I shouldn't like a child of mine to be around with that ... that young man ... all day.'

It wasn't the strict truth, but the nagging thought had been there in Howard's own mind, that Jago was not the best companion for Opal. Now, he had to do something about it, since Minerva had expressed the viewpoint. If he didn't, she would go and tell his mother about it, and his mother would fret and worry, and Gertrude would be reproachful to him for not keeping upsetting things from his mother.

He rode forward a little. 'What on earth do you think you are doing?' he thundered. He hadn't meant to raise his voice, and it startled them all. Jago, who had retrieved the ring, dropped it again. The puppy fell in the water, and Opal shrank back against Ann, almost unseating her.

Ann looked round indignantly. She had come through a very nasty time. They had found the ring and now Howard Crayne, by his stupidity and his arrogance, had made them lose it again. Ann had no patience with such things. She didn't like what she had seen of Minerva since that first dazzling evening, nor had she liked what she had heard the staff saying about her. Minerva was now smiling kindly at her, and called, 'My dear, you look very cold! Come off that rock and bring the child with you, and I do really advise you to relinquish that … that person's animals to him.'

Ann looked steadily at her, her first shock over. Now she was merely nettled. She turned her back on Minerva and said to the

118

staring Jago, 'It's all right. Go down and get it again. Then give it to me. It's a secret. Don't let them see. Go on!' so, made confident again by her tone of voice he again dived. Ann was pleased he hadn't stood there being stupid as he sometimes did. She wanted them to see how beautifully he could dive. But neither Howard nor Minerva were looking. Something had startled Minerva's horse and it danced nervously up the slope. Howard reined in and tried to catch the bridle, and had to chase after the nervous animal until he had caught it.

Jago retrieved the ring for Ann and she slipped it on her finger and Opal and she breathed a sigh of relief. 'Thank you, Jago. That was very clever of you!' Ann said firmly.

'It's a secret,' he kept on saying over and over again.

'Yes, it's a secret. I think the animals had better be a secret, too. Could you take them home and … hide them with your bird?'

Opal looked nervously at her, but Jago was all for it. He nodded fiercely, picked up his clothes, the parcel and the puppy and the kitten and went off at his jog-trot, along the edge of the now fast receding tide. Ann and the child discreetly walked up the slope after the horses, which were now still and quiet. Howard looked back, and was surprised to see only Ann and the child, walking quietly, without animals, without fuss. 'Really, Minerva,' he said, in an annoyed voice, 'I wish you hadn't said anything. There's obviously nothing wrong here! Nothing I can be cross for, anyway.'

So another storm was averted. Opal didn't catch a chill through being out so long and the animals were well fed and warm below stairs. But the kitten remembered that Ann had been the one to duck it in the sea and afterwards to cuddle it in her scarf so when Mrs Farraker came across Ann's scarf and washed it and sent a maid up to return it to her, the kitten went in the wake of the scarf and crept into Ann's room and was waiting purring on her bed when she went in to change.

'Uncle Howard won't like it,' Opal warned.

'How do you know?' Ann retorted, cuddling the tiny scrap into her neck. 'Besides, he won't know, will he? I'll let Mrs Farraker into the secret and she'll see about letting him out and getting him in.'

Opal kicked the feet of the dressing-table. 'You think she's all right, don't you?' She glanced experimentally at Ann.

Ann said, with a sideways grin. 'Oh, no, I don't. I think she's a real villainess who takes down everything I say on a secret hidden tape-recorder and takes it to play over to Mrs Crayne when my back is turned.' And she laughed aloud at the indignant and furious look the child directed at her.

'You're not supposed to tell stories like that! That's what *I* do!' Opal said, and turned her back on her.

And then, just when things seemed to be going smoothly – no trouble from Howard because of his finding them on the shore with Jago and the animals and no trouble from Mrs Farraker because of the cat – a really big storm blew up. A letter came for Ann.

'I understood you didn't have anyone to correspond with you!' Howard said coldly. It had been put by her plate at breakfast. Howard, Ann and the child were the only ones down at that hour. His mother always took breakfast in her own quarters. Minerva didn't emerge from her room so early either.

'Well, I don't say I haven't the odd friend or two, although I can't think who'd want to write to me,' Ann said in a puzzled voice.

He frowned. He wanted to know what was in that letter but he had no right to open it first. He was shocked, puzzled. What was the matter with him? Why should he care? This girl was just a stranger, with whom he was to enter into a business marriage for his own reasons. He would never need to see her more than once a week, for he was

121

scarcely ever at Kingsbride these days. So why was he worrying? What did it matter if she had a letter?

Her face cleared.

'Oh, I know what it will be! Someone's written about my trunk!'

'Your trunk! Haven't you had it sent on yet? Where is it?' Howard asked, frowning. He didn't like things to be inefficiently arranged.

'Well, I wasn't going to take it for granted that I'd got the job so I left my trunk in town, with instructions to send it on if I wanted it. Well, I did write and ask my landlady to send it on—'

Domestic details, very boring, Ann decided, watching his face, and letting her words trail off as she slit open the letter. He was watching her, still wondering who'd written, and he saw her face change. This was no landlady's letter about a trunk.

'Dear Ann,' she read to herself, and could feel her face flushing. 'I was so surprised to know you had gone, and without even saying goodbye to me. I would have come and seen you off, you know that! I think it was a bit unkind of Felicity to put you in a difficult position like that. If you'd said, you could have come and stayed at our place. I would like to hear where you are and how you are getting on, if you could spare the time to write,' and it was signed ROB.

Rob-down-the-road, Felicity had always scathingly called him. And Ann hadn't thought there was enough in that friendship to go and say goodbye. Indeed, she had been so worried about her future that she had forgotten all about him. At best, he had just been a shy young man who smiled at her and sometimes said a word or two. Felicity made a joke about him when possible.

'Well?' Howard asked sharply. 'Who is it from?'

Ann carefully put the folded letter back in the envelope and put it on the table, placing her hand on it with a final gesture. 'Just an old friend.'

Howard tightened his lips and said no more until Opal, always finished first, was fidgeting to leave the table. 'You may go, Opal. No, you stay here Ann. I want to talk to you,' he said.

Alone together, Ann waited with composure for what he wanted to say.

'I know this marriage is just a job,' he began, 'but all the same you will be my wife, so far as the outside world is concerned.'

Ann waited, still not commenting on her letter. He stared at it.

'We're not married yet,' she said at last, in a low voice. 'A job, I think you said. Well, I shall perform my side of it to the best of my ability. But it doesn't mean that I have to let

123

you see my correspondence. I don't think it would if you and I were to be properly married.'

He went rather red, then he controlled his anger with an effort. 'That is not a point that arises. Let us be civilised. Just tell me who wrote to you and then we'll forget it.'

'I will … if you will tell me what Minerva Thornton means to you and how long she is going to stay in this house and go around with you.'

Her heart beat faster as she took this enormous step. She didn't even know why she had, or why she should suddenly care about his being on a horse beside Minerva, yet Ann who he was going to marry should be walking with the child, and getting reprimanded by that woman in her syrupy voice.

'That doesn't concern you,' he said, his jaw tightening.

'Then my correspondence doesn't concern you,' she said with politeness. 'It is my own affair, as people like Minerva Thornton are your affair. But this district is interested in the people in this house. Don't blame me if everyone talks about your odd marriage to me.'

'Why should they?' He flung up his head, really angry now.

'But you must know – I know, and I've never had servants before. You must know that they know everything that goes on upstairs and they gossip all over the place. You can't stop them.'

He scraped back his chair and came round the room to pull her chair back. 'Get up! Look at me, Ann!' So she did, although it cost her an effort. Increasingly she was finding it vaguely upsetting when she tried to meet his glance. She told herself it was because his eyes had such a piercing quality but now she wasn't sure that that was so.

'Every time I consider you,' he said, 'you seem much more suited to be my wife than I had at first thought. And yet I get the feeling that increasingly you are coming to doubt the wisdom of this marriage.'

'That's true,' she said. 'I think I'd feel better about it if you'd tell me the truth, what exactly is behind it. You must have a good reason for wanting such a marriage – or is it so you can be secure to flirt with people like Minerva and not have to marry her?' she said, anger driving her.

He didn't like that a bit. 'You have no right to say that!'

'Yes, I have. Every right. I'm going to be your wife and you said it was absolutely legal and binding. I haven't asked you much about it but … supposing, just supposing … well, what I mean is, with an ordinary marriage, if one partner dies, the other inherits everything. Well, I am a sane reasonable person and I want to know where I stand if … I were to be widowed.'

'You would inherit most of what I possess, of course. There would be other bene-ficiaries, principally Opal. You must realise that.'

'Opal! Well, of course, that's all right, poor child.'

'Who did you think would inherit?' he asked twistedly.

He was still holding her hands. She tried to take them away but he held them more tightly. 'I didn't think. It's all so queer and strange,' she said at last. 'Am I really doing the right thing? Well, Opal is happy about it, so yes, I suppose it's as right as it can be in the circumstances.'

'Yes, it is chiefly for Opal's sake,' he reiter-ated. 'Though I sometimes think…' and he broke off and looked at her in puzzled fashion.

'What do you sometimes think?' she asked with a catch of the breath.

'That even though it is just a job, where you are concerned, not a proper marriage, I mean – well, we might get something out of it, you and I. Something like friendship, I mean. Well, bless me, what's a friend? Some-one to interest, stimulate, be there to talk to or ask advice? I think you would be very good in that role. I don't see why I shouldn't benefit so far as friendship is concerned, and if you could find anything of the sort in my power to offer you…' He trailed off, uncertain. It bothered him. He was never uncertain, as a rule.

'I think I should like that,' she said primly. 'Friendship, yes, it might be nice. We haven't tried it yet,' she finished with a quirk of a smile.

It amused him. 'I think you'd be quite fun to have around,' he told her. 'I'd suffer, of course. Well, there's an old saying, about the husband finding his situation a sweet tyranny, because he endures his torments willingly.'

That was a retrograde step. Ann was well read and he hadn't realised to the full. She said coolly, 'I feel that doesn't apply to us. I know the saying. You misquoted. It should have been, "Love is a sweet tyranny, because the lover endurth his torments willingly." It just doesn't apply.'

She tried to pull away from him and the penetrating look in his eyes as he closed the distance between them. 'That isn't to say it couldn't apply, at some time, if we didn't fight too much, don't you think?' he murmured. Now he had her hands held flat against his chest, and she could feel the strong beat of his heart, banging away in a tempo not quite as fast as her own, but near it. 'You have the sort of personality that penetrates quite slowly, insidiously,' he told her, 'and before folk realise it, you've taken people over. You came here quietly, and nothing was the same again. I tried not to let it change anything. I kept telling myself it was just a business arrangement for purposes that … were quite important to me. And I assured myself that my bachelor state – my happy bachelor state – need not be disturbed.'

'And you want to go on believing that. Well, if you let go of my hands, and sit on the far side of the table and retreat behind your newspaper,' she said fiercely, 'things can be just as they were. Don't shake your head at me. They can be, I assure you! I just want it to be a job. I'm quite satisfied … at least, I would be, if you didn't ask about my letters.'

Jealousy flared within him again. Someone had written to her and she hadn't disclosed who it was. 'A husband has the right to know,' he insisted. 'It's that Tom Westbury, isn't it? Confess it!'

'I will not, because it wasn't from him, and what's the good of stipulating that a person must have been jilted if you're going to be always suspecting that the former lover will try and contact a person again?'

'I don't know,' he admitted. 'I had no idea I would care one way or the other. Well, I don't care, of course. At least, I wouldn't, if you'd just say. Why can't you just say who that letter was from? How can we be friends if you're not going to be frank with me?'

The endearing look she kept for Opal, Jago and the animals had fled and she was withdrawn, and yet infinitely alluring. He must find out who had written to her. He was shocked at how badly he wanted to know. 'You must tell me, Ann!'

'No, and you can't make me. You are keeping your life behind a wall, so I shall keep mine. That's fair, you must admit.'

There was a sort of suspended moment of time, in which Ann wondered just what he would do after that daring speech of hers. But she never found out, for Minerva, who should have been taking breakfast in her room and not emerging until after ten, appeared at the door, a smile of pure amusement on her lips. 'Whatever is going on?' she asked, as if they were not engaged.

SEVEN

Ann made a discovery in that moment. She found that Minerva would be just the kind of person one could hate quickly and easily. Ann was shocked at herself. She had never felt like it towards anyone before. Not even towards Howard. He made her nettled, furiously angry at times, but there was a warmth in that anger. Minerva was so sly, with that kind smile of hers, but the dagger-thrust of the things she had to say.

Ann said sweetly, 'Not a thing is the matter. I am going, anyway. You may have your old friend Howard all to yourself for a while,' and grinning at Howard, she took herself out of the room, with her letter.

That letter she tore into shreds and disposed of, at once. She wouldn't, not for anything, give Howard the pleasure of knowing he had forced her to show it to him. And she wasn't going to leave anything so personal around in this house. Without quite knowing how, she suddenly felt that nothing was sacred.

She looked for Opal. They must plan something right away, before she started being cross again at the way Minerva appeared on the scene so suddenly, without warning. By the time she had found Opal, however, a maid came up with a message: Howard had decided to take both Ann and the child out for the day.

Opal looked in dismay at Ann. 'I don't want to go out with *him*,' she said.

Ann dismissed the girl with a message to say they would be ready as soon as they could, and took Opal's hands. 'Neither do I, but as I've got some things lined up for us to do, let's do this duty outing with a bit of dignity, shall we? After all, if we don't make a fuss, we are not likely to be stopped doing the things I've planned. That's common sense, isn't it?' So Opal agreed.

Howard had the Land Rover ready by the time they went down. He looked at them rather critically, she thought. Opal wore a nice new yellow sweater over brown trousers, and Ann wore a blue sweater over navy slacks. They had raincoats with them. Sensibly dressed, quickly, too, and no fuss or cumbersome parcels. Not even a camera, which he abhorred. It made people look like tourists, he considered, and it always annoyed him. 'Good! Both on time. Well, I had in mind rather a treat. We are going to a place called Venfold. It's very old and quaint, and a lot to see and do.' He looked critically at Opal, and she glared back at him. Ann held her breath, wondering what on earth to say, to stop a new storm brewing, but Howard merely smiled swiftly, helped them both into the car, and drove quietly away. Ann drew a deep breath of relief, for Minerva hadn't appeared.

It was a wonderful day, after all. When Howard liked to put himself out he could be rather nice to be with, Ann saw, and Opal gave herself up to enjoying herself after a while. That was a relief too. Ann couldn't help wondering why Opal had decided to have fun and not make a fuss, but it was so nice when she wasn't making a fuss.

Howard drove along narrow lanes, stopping every time there was a view of the sea through some gap in the cliffs, or where the trees broke and showed a breathtaking landscape, as this county seemed to do, all the time.

'How will you feel about living here, Ann?' Howard asked, after they had had a satisfying lunch in a restaurant that was on the first floor of a black-timbered white house that leaned slightly towards the house facing it, over a narrow street of extremely interesting shops. Everyone in their little party had eaten just a bit too much. Opal had finished with one ice cream too many and looked rather dopey, Ann thought, with some amusement. The question caught her off balance, and she said, 'Oh, I'll love it.'

She blushed as she caught his steady look.

'I presume you mean how will I like the county for a home background,' she amended with dignity. 'I think – I always have thought – that it was an enchanting corner of England in which to live, and I still think so. That is what you asked me, isn't it?'

'I think you know what I meant,' Howard said quietly. 'The word "here" meant not only the county but our village of Regent's Bay, our house – Kingsbride – and our family. You will be Mrs Howard Crayne,' he said, finishing there although she got the feeling he hadn't meant to. His glance had slipped down to her engagement ring and for one startled moment she wondered if one of the stones was missing, or that some other evidence of its dip in the sea showed for him to see. She tore her glance from it and looked at Opal, but Opal had gone to sleep.

It might have been funny, but just at that moment, everything seemed very quiet. She glanced round. Almost all the other diners had gone, the waitresses were at the far end talking quietly among themselves while they waited for Ann's party to finish, and now the child was asleep, it was just herself and Howard.

He pushed the point home further by sliding his hand across the table and over hers, but whether it was to possess her hand or to point to the ownership of that extremely valuable ring she couldn't be sure.

Her heart thumped painfully. 'It's a business arrangement,' she reminded him. 'I wish you would allow it to stay that way.' And as he didn't answer or change his expression, she said breathlessly, 'Just for the moment. Don't rush me!' which wasn't what she had meant to say at all.

Opal woke up at that moment and the spell was broken. 'What's going on?' the child demanded. 'Why are you two looking at each other like that? Have you had a row?'

She was still half asleep or she wouldn't have risked that. But the waitress came back at that moment and Howard's small tight smile betrayed nothing of how he had met that instant juvenile reaction. He didn't even try to catch Ann's eye, which she had feared. In moments like this, a flare of belligerence against him arose in her, threatening to choke her. She thought it was a natural defence of young Opal that she was experiencing, but in her heart she knew that wasn't really so. But she wasn't willing to examine the sensation yet.

'What are we going to do now?' Opal demanded, stumbling outside into the bright sunshine with a sulky frown on her face. She had been caught sleeping, and as always was rather difficult afterwards.

Howard avoided Ann's anxious glance at

him and said smoothly, 'We'll take a look and see what Venfold has to offer, and you may do anything you like!'

Such a rash promise silenced both Ann and the child, so they walked soberly by his side through the quaint narrow streets, eschewed toy shops but stared in fascination at a display in a bulbous shop window, designed to tempt the angler; stayed a shade too long looking at the gear for water sports, Opal longingly admiring a pair of flippers much too big for her, and shooting past, with distaste, a shop with everything for the horse rider. That smacked too much of Minerva. There was an extremely old and musty little church which Opal wanted to see inside, in case of things coming out of old tombs, she said.

Howard raised his brows and looked at Ann, who shook her head helplessly but plunged into the icy and very musty gloom behind Opal. Howard dutifully bought booklets about the church when they had looked their fill and emerged into strong sunlight. And then, at the end of the main shopping street, they came out into a twisty road down to a perfect natural harbour. 'Venfold's pride and joy,' Howard said quietly. 'Everything for the small owner of sail boats, nothing to tempt people who want sand on which to leave litter, and sunbathe all day. Venfold just isn't that sort of place.'

And he looked thoughtfully at Opal. 'There is just enough breeze to tempt me to take out the *Venfold Darling*. Want to go?'

They couldn't believe it. 'You mean ... you want to take us out in a sail-boat?' Ann gasped, and Opal's small quaint face was creased up into open yet pleasurable disbelief. Her eyes batted fiercely behind her glasses, and Howard thought, with another of those odd feelings, that the child, in her doubt and anticipation, had literally thrown herself against Ann's side and was hanging on to her, as if to be sustained through yet another disappointment. Ann was perfect for leaning on in such a situation. Again he asked himself, as he formally assured them both that he had indeed meant what he said, what on earth had made that chap jilt Ann? He would come back, of course, realise what an ass he had been, and take Ann from them. Then he tried to think how any man could jilt her, anyway. And the thought struck him that she didn't look as if she'd been jilted. There was no deep hurt in her eyes, and he didn't think she was all that good at hiding her feelings. But there it was: the chap had jilted her and that was why she was here.

He left the thought, and answered with some amusement her question as to the little craft's name. 'Well, it is an idiotic name, I agree, but it was already there when

I bought her, and I'm superstitious about changing a name. What's wrong with it, anyway? It suggests a love of a boat, and that what she is,' and he looked hard at Ann, as if, Opal thought resentfully, he was meaning something else, nothing to do with the boat at all. That was the trouble with adults. They said words you knew, but they made them mean different things. She hunched her shoulders, but Ann pulled her back and said, 'Well, never mind about the name, I personally would love a little trip on a day like this and I don't care if I *do* get seasick!' which had the effect of sweeping enormous relief through Opal, who had only once been on the sea – a rough grey sea in a row-boat – with some other people she didn't know very well who had offered to take her to the seaside for the day. She had been ill, and never forgotten it.

Howard led them down to where the *Venfold Darling* was moored, and Ann helped, under his instructions, to make her ready. Opal, watching, thought there was an awful lot to be done in order to take a little trip out in a small boat with a bit of a sail, but she wisely kept quiet, listening instead to instructions about the sheet (why couldn't Uncle Howard say 'rope') and minding the boom, which appeared to be the wood thing through the bottom of the sail, which swung about in the most alarming way. Why couldn't he nail it to the side of the boat? Then Opal saw that the wind and the rudder were responsible for the boom swinging and wisely ducked and hunched herself into a little ball, well below the reach of anything that moved in her direction. But when Opal crouched and kept small and silent, she was at her most deadly. She watched the other two, rather than the beautiful shoreline slipping away. It was Howard's constant returning keen gaze to Ann and every movement she made, rather than the glittering diamonds of sun on unseasonable blue sea that Opal watched. She thought resentfully that Howard must have planned this trip; he had hastily changed into a rough sweater and handed out thin waterproof garments and life jackets for them all and the old man who had helped them cast off had seemed to expect them, the way he told them they had weather for 'this' trip, as if it were something special, and the old man looked at Ann with tender approval. They all knew she was to marry Howard, Opal thought, her resentment mounting. Ann was hers, she told herself. Everything she had, someone took it away, sooner or later. Cheated, she sat and watched them until the spray messed up her glasses and she couldn't see anything but was too miserable to remove them and clean them up.

It was Ann who came and did that later, when they were out a good way and Howard had lashed enough things down to manage on his own. He stood easily, half watching the sea and sky, half watching Opal's tight little face as Ann removed her glasses. 'Poor scrap,' Ann murmured, 'you're not enjoying this very much, are you?' and Opal perversely said, 'Yes, I am, and I'm not seasick!'

Ann absently sat with a loose arm round her, looking at a gull's antics up above their little mast, and wondering why she was so 'high' with happiness today. She cautioned herself; there had been rare happy times in the past, but always they seemed to end up, at the close of day, in disaster.

It was this sense of approaching doom, as she derisively called it to herself, that stayed with her, under her gaiety and obvious enjoyment of the trip. Howard complimented her on her crewmanship, and her level-headedness. His eyes told her he liked a lot of other things about her, too.

'Where's that ole Minerva? Why didn't she try to push in too?' Opal asked, spoiling the day with a suddenness that Ann flinched from.

'Don't let's think of that, pet,' she said hastily. 'Don't let's mention her, because there are some more nice things in store for us.'

Opal wouldn't be mollified. Howard

accepted, without surprise, that Opal didn't like the trip in the neat little sail craft, because he could see that Ann had enjoyed it very much, especially being the crew for a while. What did a child like Opal really want, he wondered, but obstinately wouldn't ask Ann. He wanted to think it out for himself. So when they had returned to shore, he drove them on to Venfold East, which was a newish addition to the old place, with a park and a small zoo, a fairground with a Big Wheel, and a lot of other things guaranteed to upset a very large lunch, and quantities of rather sickly ice cream concoctions which Ann refused to interfere with. Opal was beginning to thaw visibly, when two things happened. Someone sitting near made a remark about 'that nice young couple and their little girl' which seemed to incense the child very much, and make Howard's jaw tighten, and then Howard pursued an arrangement he had made earlier that day by telephone and took them to procure a dog and a cat for Opal. A pedigree Bedlington terrier from the same kennels as his mother's dogs (thereby winning his mother's thin approval) and a supercilious Siamese cat, half grown from kittenhood, to again appease his mother, who expected animals to be housetrained and out of the mischievous stage. Opal's face crumpled but she refused to cry. 'I don't like them. I don't want them,' she said thickly, but nonetheless clearly.

Howard, who wasn't used to thinking things out carefully when making a gift, looked as if someone had struck him a blow in the face. He whitened, and Ann felt like crying herself. Whatever good had been done that day, was all swept aside by Opal's words. But Howard should have known, Ann felt; he should have understood that mongrels with tin cans on their tails, and half-starved kittens whose only endearing quality was their utter mischief, was all Opal cared about.

'What was the matter with my gift?' he asked, as they left the kennels in an atmosphere of frost all round. To cancel such an order was not likely to be popular, even with the Crayne family. Besides, Howard felt foolish, and somehow let-down. 'What is it she would have liked? Surely not a poodle! After all, my mother has to be considered!'

Ann couldn't tell him the truth.

'Would you have liked them?' he demanded, with belated inspiration.

'I'm sure you'd like me to be candid,' she said primly. 'No, I'm afraid I wouldn't.'

'I thought you were both animal lovers!' he snapped.

'I'll explain, as soon as I can think of–' and she broke off, going pink.

'As soon as you can think of a way to

explain to an imbecile who thinks he only has to get out his cheque book and arrange for a gift? Is that it?'

Her heart bled for him. Undoubtedly that was all he had been wanted for in the past; to open his cheque book. She shook her head. 'When you are Opal's age...' she began, then broke off again. He would have been a normal boy at a normal school where people had a set pattern of gifts and pets. Anyone who had stepped out of line would have been considered very odd, and out of other folks' circle. She shook her head. 'With Opal, who has apparently not had a happy or stable life, I imagine,' but he broke in harshly, 'How would *you* know?'

She looked squarely at him. 'I know because it's my job to get to know Opal, and in doing so, I get scraps of information, impressions, from things said or things left unsaid. It entails a lot of patience, stemming from liking the child and wanting to know her. One day she'll actually give me a confidence of what she remembers. At least, I pray she will,' she said, half under her breath.

After a frosty return journey, they swept in the back way to enter the garage. She left him, staring at her with a hunger in his eyes which was apparent even to the child, who trailed after Ann, only waiting till they were out of sight of her irate guardian, to fling herself on Ann. 'It was rotten of him!' Opal stormed. 'Why didn't he ask me what sort of dog and cat I'd like? Not just *give* them to me! What *he* thought I *ought* to like!'

'Well, the age, health and pedigree of the animal has to be gone into and the price, and forms to be filled in, all sorts of things,' Ann hastily explained. 'Not just like going to a pet shop to buy a mongrel, or having one from the litter of a neighbour's dog, as people I used to know always did.'

Opal hung on her arm. 'Tell me about the people you used to know.'

They progressed by way of back stairs and uncarpeted passages, to the top floor, their own little domain, Opal skipping a little, and gaining comfort from the warm touch of Ann's arm under her clutching young fingers, Ann walking in her usual moderate pace, carefully picking her words. 'People who lived in a street of houses all alike, with back gardens and little front gardens. Kennels in the back garden for a big guard sort of dog, or a dog basket in the kitchen for a small one – and the dog usually crept upstairs to sleep at the foot of the owner's bed,' Ann broke off with a warm smile, that set Opal nodding.

'Yes, like I read in a book,' she said. So that didn't ring a bell. Ann sighed, and went on talking, but Opal suddenly broke in, 'This is a rotten day really. It's going to finish up nasty. Well, I don't know, of course I don't. I'm just guessing. Or perhaps I was the seventh child of the seventh child of a witch. Yes, I reckon that's what I was. That's how I know there are people walking about in this house at night who have no business to be.'

'Ghosts and ghoulies,' Ann agreed amiably, having discovered that the child wanted indignation and a ticking off, and felt cheated if you agreed with her or capped her wild stories. Today, however, she merely looked pinched and miserable and said, 'Uncle Howard likes you. He likes you an awful lot. He keeps looking at you. I hate him when he looks at you like that. You're mine, not his.'

Ann's heart sank. What could she say? The child was unhappy again. She did her best, talking fast, but she knew she had lost, when Opal appeared later in the dirtiest old jersey and torn jeans (probably hidden away somewhere against such an occasion and situation) and with her newly cropped hair standing up on end and mud on her face. Belligerence oozed out of every pore. She stared at Ann.

'Aren't you going to say anything?' she demanded at last, but Ann shook her head. 'No, if you want to go around looking like that, I suppose you'd better, but don't come near me, will you, because I'm clean at the moment.'

Opal looked stormy. 'I heard voices in the air,' she said experimentally.

Ann said nothing, but continued with going through books for their next lesson; it would have to be next morning now.

Opal tried shock tactics. 'I heard that ole Minerva telling Uncle Howard rotten things about you.'

'I'm not surprised,' Ann said coolly. 'She doesn't like me. I expect she's like that to anyone she doesn't like, and she won't like to think I'm going to marry him, I expect.'

'You're not, I shouldn't wonder, not after what she said,' Opal drew a deep breath to announce. That really had an effect.

Ann threw her head up, left the books alone, and said quietly, 'You'd better tell me just what you heard, no frills, no made-up bits, because I might have to do something about it. And no voices-in-the-air business either.'

Opal wavered. 'I was just walking down the Dark Corridor,' which was what she called the always empty corridor leading to Mrs Crayne's suite. 'And I heard it, all around me. Honest! And she was telling Uncle Howard that your chap had turned up today – the one who was supposed to have jilted you! You didn't tell the truth about what jilting meant, did you?'

'I told you enough for then,' Ann said. 'You wouldn't have understood.'

'No, and I don't understand now, not why you said you were jilted and you're not! That ole Minerva said you'd not been jilted nor nothing – it was all a pack of lies! That's what made Uncle Howard so wild. He said he couldn't trust you any more than the other two people who came here.'

'Now just a minute,' Ann said, going round the table to the child. What she was saying had the ring of truth about it.

Opal backed away. 'It's not my fault. I was miserable and I wanted someone to see me like this – all dirty – so I thought I'd go down to their part of the house and that's where you can hear things. I don't know how you can. No, it isn't listening at key-holes – if you looked at those doors you'd see there weren't any keyholes. They're big heavy doors with bolts inside, just like they used to be, Mrs Farraker said.'

Side-tracked for the moment, Ann said, 'Are they? Are you sure?' and racked her brains to remember what Mrs Crayne's door had been like, but she couldn't remember. She had been so angry on that occasion.

'Yes, of course I'm sure,' Opal said scornfully.

'Then, if you're so sure of your facts, just tell me what name Mrs Thornton gave to the man who was supposed to have jilted me, and how she came to know anything about

146

it,' and her voice was dangerously quiet.

Opal and gone too far to retract now, and besides, the child in this wretched mood was rather apt to go to the brink of danger without being able to help it. She said firmly, 'Tom Westbury, she said, and she knew because he came here when we were out and she asked him lots of things and … and he told her,' she gasped, backing away in fear, and finally taking to her heels.

She shut herself in her bedroom and sat shivering on the window-seat. What could she have said that was so important that Ann had gone white as a sheet and gripped a pencil so hard that it had snapped in two?

EIGHT

Mrs Crayne looked up under hooded eyes and said to Gertrude, 'You don't like it? Why? Has that milksop girl Ann won you over as she has other people?'

Gertrude, who was allowed a certain amount of liberty in speech, and knowing full well that her mistress couldn't really do without her, said quietly, 'Milksop she may be, but I can't help being pleased that poor child Opal has found someone to give her a bit of comfort and affection, madam.'

'You don't think dear Minerva could?' Mrs Crayne suggested softly.

Gertrude said calmly, 'I think just the same as you do about Mrs Thornton's manner with children, madam,' which made Mrs Crayne scowl.

'Well, it doesn't matter. The child will go away to school anyway. And don't remind me of the reason why it is thought in some quarters better for her not to go. We don't know. It hasn't been tried. It should be tried, and if it doesn't work because of a certain reason, then there are other arrangements that could be made. Well, it's no use looking at me like that, Gertrude – I can't stand that child about. Those eyes behind those glasses, always looking. And the ears – I imagine they actually flap, she listens so hard to everything. Everything!'

'Your own niece's child, madam,' Gertrude reproached.

'Kindly don't refer to her birth again, Gertrude!' Mrs Crayne snapped.

'Mr Howard constantly keeps it in mind,' Gertrude said hastily. She didn't care. Sometimes she was half decided to leave Mrs Crayne, retire on her savings, ready to come back to Ann, who, as Howard's wife, might well want her some day. Mrs Crayne was furious. 'How did you know she was Elaine's child? I never told you!'

'I can't remember how I got the impression, madam, but you didn't deny it just now, though I wasn't sure,' Gertrude said, and went out of the room quickly before Mrs Crayne could explode with wrath. She hated to feel that her maid's baitings got the answers she wanted, without having to ask the question in so many words. Really, if only she could find someone to replace Gertrude, she would, this very day!

Gertrude came back into the room, busy about her duties. Mrs Crayne said, stiffly, having decided it was bad for her to get worked up, 'And kindly see that Mrs Thornton doesn't find out. I mean to see her married to my son. He likes her and she wants him. He needs her fortune, too.'

'She'll find out,' Gertrude warned. 'She's working on it. Saying the wrong to get the right.'

'Well, she mustn't know!'

'She might find out. Too many people have worked it out that she wasn't the one that Mr Howard pines over, though it was put about at the time of their quarrel, that he was all broken up over her and nobody else,' Gertrude said, delivering her master stroke.

She was sorry though. Mrs Crayne seemed to shrink a little. 'Are you all right, madam?' she asked softly, going down on her knees beside the chair.

'Yes,' Mrs Crayne sighed, which was alarming because she usually dramatised herself even if she was well. 'I just feel rather spent and … futile sometimes. I should have let him marry his cousin, but I didn't believe in alliances between first cousins. Things couldn't have been much worse, as they did turn out, though. But no, I will not let myself believe it was my fault!' she said, rallying. 'And you are not to kneel by me with all that sympathy oozing out of you, Gertrude, and trapping me into giving confidences I shall be sorry for. Get up with you! And don't encourage that girl Ann. I shall clear her out of here somehow, and soon! I don't like her. She's my enemy,

150

because she's implacable. *And Howard is looking at her like he used to look at Elaine,* her thoughts mocked her.

She got up and went to her window. Ann was hurrying through the gardens to the way through the orchard. Her back view looked decidedly angry. She had just had a row with Howard. Now, shocked at the things they had said (shouted!) at each other, she felt as near tears as she had ever been. Her anger had flared because he had presumed that what he had heard was right. It probably was but he might have had the patience and courtesy and the common sense to ask for her version which would undoubtedly have been different from Minerva's.

'I thought I could trust you!' he had stormed. 'You said – you repeated – that you had been jilted, when I asked you! You even gave his name!'

'That was all your fault, for putting in such a silly advertisement!'

'Don't shout at me!' the arrogant Howard had fumed. 'You answered the advertisement and told a lie over it. You had no right to come here if you weren't complying with all the conditions.'

'You should have taken up the information I gave you! You said you would – why didn't you? Couldn't be bothered? It would have lowered your dignity?'

'No, I just thought you looked like a

person who told the truth. Now I know you can't, I'll never trust you again.'

'Why bother? You won't have the chance, since I shan't be here!'

'Good heavens, you don't think I should call off our marriage, now everything is settled?' That made him even more angry. 'I am just asking you, begging you, to consider the truth next time, and not tell me a pack of lies.'

'And who told you about this? Dear Minerva?' Her anger was sinking her to the depths of silly cut and thrust and she knew it and despised herself for it. It was so horrible to come at a time like this, after today, when they had seemed to get closer. And besides, there was Opal to consider.

'The chap came with your trunk. A fellow doesn't make a journey all this way to bring a trunk, which could have been put on a train,' Howard said bitterly, but he was remembering what Minerva had told him; that the young man had been intrigued rather than put out, to think that Ann had used his name, remembered him at all. 'She uses any man. You can see she's like that. And all the time she pretends to be so innocent, so uncontaminated by the male sex,' Minerva had said. Howard had caught a glimpse of the big rangy Tom Westbury himself.

Now he watched Ann's face for reaction.

Her anger lifted and a warm smile appeared briefly. 'Oh, did he?' she said. 'He always was such a decent sort. He shouldn't have been treated like that! Oh, I don't mean by my saying he'd jilted me. He'd laugh at that, I expect. If you must know, he was crazy about my beautiful cousin, and she was the one who wouldn't marry him because of his job in Scotland, and she was the one who did any jilting that was to be done. Now are you satisfied? Well, I had to have a story, didn't I? Because I needed this job so badly. But I've just discovered I don't need it at all. I'm leaving. Now!'

'You will not leave!' he had thundered. 'You have given your word and this time there will be no dishonesty. There is a marriage contracted for, and you're going through with it. And why did you need this job so badly?'

He fancied he saw dislike in her sensitive young face.

'You wouldn't understand if I told you, Howard Crayne, because you've never been without a roof over your head, nor had to smart because a close relative had tricked you into being homeless and didn't seem to think it was a bad thing. You haven't had to suffer anything!' but that was going too far.

He was round the room in no time and caught her by the shoulders. 'I would have you know that I have plumbed the depths of suffering. Oh, yes, I agree I have a family home that has housed many generations of my people. Oh, yes, I am not short of a bit of cash though I am not as rich as you think I am. But I know what suffering is, and not trusting people...' He looked hungrily at her. 'I thought I had found someone who had warmth under her lovely face, and not a heart of ice. For heaven's sake tell me I'm wrong or I'll never trust anyone again.'

She was powerless to do anything. There was that curious excitement racing through her, and she couldn't move to escape his face coming down to hers, nor his hard angry mouth taking her soft lips in a kiss that devoured her. It seemed to last for hours, yet it could only have been seconds, for he thrust her away, a curious look on his white face, and he muttered: 'I'm sorry. I shouldn't have...' and he turned and strode over to the window to stare out moodily at the gardens. 'You'd better go,' he said, without turning. 'Good heavens, yes, and if you can do something to that child – she couldn't be more filthy! Get her in and give her a bath or something!' So Ann escaped, still bemused, simmering with anger beneath.

Mrs Farraker was taking Opal upstairs. Neither of them saw Ann, so strong was the altercation between them, neither listening to the other but hurling insults at each other, voicing the dislike they both professed. Ann sighed.

No point in butting in there. She went out through a side door and felt the cool breeze on her hot cheeks. To get away for a time and think over all that. Why was he insisting on the queer marriage if he didn't trust her and had discovered she hadn't been jilted? The child was right in her information but how had Opal discovered it? And Minerva – what did she hope to gain by driving Ann and Howard apart, since he was clearly not contemplating altering his plans for the future?

She strode through the orchard, unaware of Mrs Crayne watching her from her window. Mrs Crayne saw Tom Westbury emerge from the shadows, and saw Ann's start of surprise. Tom took her hands and gave her a casual neighbourly kiss on the cheek but to Mrs Crayne it looked the sort of kiss she wanted exchanged so she could hold it as another black mark against Ann. But all Tom said was, 'Well, it's good to see you, lass! You're a caution, telling that tale to get this job! No, of course I'm not wild! Intrigued, amused, maybe, but most of all I'm just furious with Felicity for treating you like that. Oh, yes, I've heard about the way she got you out of the flat. I told her what I thought of her, much good did it do me. Never mind, lass, tell me all about it and what's going to happen to you. I hope it won't get you into trouble, me still being on their land but to tell you the truth, I hung about to try and speak to you, and then I got a bit lost. Rambling old place, isn't it?' A long speech, understandingly rambling, because he could see that Ann was near tears. It gave her time to recover.

He put his arms round her shoulders and walked by her side. She gulped and said, shakily, 'Oh, Tom, I'm so glad you've come. I need a friend. Someone to lean on. I'm in such an awful mess!'

'Well, I gathered that, lass.' He smiled down at her. He was as tall as Howard Crayne but he hadn't Howard's lithe grace of movement laced with arrogance. It was queer. Tom was so nice. Ann remembered how nice she had always thought him – too nice for Felicity – but now he didn't measure up so well beside Howard Crayne. Tom was nice in an ordinary sort of way and (although she had no great liking for Howard Crayne) she found herself thinking that Howard was nice in a rather special sort of way. You might feel like fighting him most of the time (as she did!) but you had to accord him respect. He didn't make a fool of himself, he had, usually, rather terrific self control considering what he had to put up with, and he was capable and knowledgeable. She tried to find other things about him but it all tied up with his being important and special, and try as she would, she couldn't change that estimation.

'It's this Howard Crayne,' she said savagely.

Tom looked quickly at her but said nothing, so she went on, 'What have you heard about it? This job, I mean?'

Tom pulled a face. He waited while Ann undid the tall door in the orchard wall and they went through into the paddocks, and then out on to common land and the buffeting wind from the sea. Then he said, 'Well, you know me. I don't like talking behind people's backs, nor saying things about young women, but that's a right one you've got there, that Mrs Thornton!'

'Minerva! Did you meet her?' Ann was surprised and crestfallen. So it was true, Opal's story! Quite true. What on earth had made Minerva speak to a casual visitor such as Tom? But almost before he spoke, Ann guessed.

'That woman wanted to do you an injury, Ann. Seems to me she thinks you and your boss are pretty well fixed up right and tight and she wants him and means to bust the thing apart before you can get married. Do you want to marry him, Ann? Because if you don't, if it's because you're alone, there's always me. I'd be glad to marry you.'

She flushed. 'Tom, how can you say such

157

a thing after the way I've used you? Besides, you are in love with Felicity, and goodness knows, she treated you badly enough!'

He smiled, a little tightly, Ann thought. 'Your beautiful cousin Felicity gets into a chap's blood. I suppose, if she wanted to come back to me...' He let his words trail off, and stood for a moment looking down at the sheer utter beauty of the breakers swirling into a cove of jagged upstanding rocks, pitting their might against rock and cliff, brief impact, flying spray backwards, and then, defeated, the sea called back its advance guard with a sucking hiss of utter rage and disappointment before gathering strength to return to the attack. It seemed to fascinate Tom. 'I shan't see that sort of thing for a long time. I suppose that's why I fixed Cornwall for my holiday. I'll be honest with you. It wasn't to see you, Ann. Then I heard you were here and needed your trunk and it seemed a good idea to bring it, see you got it safely, and see how you were faring. I've been worrying about you since Felicity...' He sighed. 'Oh, well, things haven't worked out too badly apparently.' He took Ann's shoulders. 'You don't look as unhappy as I expected. In fact, you look as if the job interested you, even though it's got its queer side to it.'

'How queer?' Ann asked cautiously.

'Well, that Mrs Thornton told me that

Crayne has got to marry in a hurry in order to get a pretty big sum of money and it's all tied up with having a wife to be responsible for a kid who's a bit queer in the head. I don't mind telling you, Ann, that when I caught on that you'd been selected for the job, I was so upset and worried that I heartily wished I hadn't been so frank with her and let her get out of me that there was no engagement and no jilting. But of course she'd asked me bluntly by then. I'd have said I was going to be engaged to you again and taken you away!'

'Big sum of money?' Ann repeated. 'But I've never heard about that. And as to Opal being not right in the head, that's a wicked lie! Oh, of course she's an odd child, spins the most awful exaggerated stories – some children do, especially the lonely ones – and she dramatises everything, but she's all right, honestly, Tom, and … I like her! And it's wicked of Minerva to say such things.'

'Well, lass, there it is. She says she doesn't know why Crayne is going ahead with the marriage now she's come back because she's got enough money for three people, double that number, she said!'

'Yes, I think that's true, but I don't think Howard is concerned all that much with money. But I can't see why he doesn't marry her now she's free because they say he was going to marry her at one time, and she left him when this very rich man turned up.'

'Maybe he's scared she'll do it again. I would be,' he said. 'Ann, think, lass – it is a very queer position. I never did like the sound of juggling with marriage vows. With me, it's for always, and because two people like each other and respect each other. Not because of a business arrangement to get money. That's all wrong.'

'Yes, I think so too, but it goes deeper than that, Tom.'

'How, lass? Don't say you've fallen in love with this arrogant beggar!'

She didn't answer that, and wished her cheeks wouldn't burn when she thought of Howard Crayne. 'It's the child, Tom. Poor little Opal. She's taken to me. She's terrified that she'll get Minerva for a stepmother. She wants me. You see, when I have married Howard, I shall have full care of Opal. She won't be sent away to a school, as one would expect.'

'As one would expect,' he repeated. 'Yes, rich folk set a store by getting rid of their young 'uns to boarding school. Right heathen aspect, I call it. My kids would have to be at home, where I could see they were all right. They could come to me with their problems. Kids always have problems to talk over. Who do they go to at boarding school, I should like to know?'

'Well, that applies especially to Opal, Tom.

She's been shunted about so much among strangers, I gather, that she flinches from going to anyone else new. She wants to be at home with us. Well, with me. She's a bit scared of her uncle, though she understands that he's her guardian and she's got to put up with him.'

'And you're willing to put up with him, instead of having … the devotion of some chap who isn't rich but will make a nice little home for you? Ann, Kingsbride isn't a home. It's a … well, like something one goes to view on a Sunday out. It couldn't be a home. It's too big and cold and … important, I suppose. You couldn't let the smell of frying chips go through the house, not a house like that. And it's too big to go to a window and call in your husband to his dinner. The gardener wouldn't like that, anyway.'

She smiled tenderly at him, but he couldn't know she was trying to picture a little house with Howard Crayne as the husband in rolled up shirt sleeves, putting down his broad paint brush and viewing the wood-work he'd been busy on, or cleaning up his fork and spade and taking a last look at the newly turned earth in the vegetable patch. She couldn't, of course, see Howard in such a role, but oddly enough, she did get a warm glowing feeling about Kingsbride with Howard on a cold winter's night, Howard standing back to a huge log fire, a glass in one hand, the books all around him, his ancestor's portraits on the walls, and Ann and the child going in to dinner with him, and belonging. There wasn't any ceremony at Kingsbride any more, as there was only Mrs Farraker and the daily girls to run the place, but still they did things with style, a quiet careful regarding of the proprieties, a feverish urge not to let standards slip even though times had changed and there wasn't much money or service to be had. And Tom was wrong in one thing. He had said Kingsbride wasn't a home and could never be. He was very wrong – Kingsbride *was* a home. It was big, cold and important, it was true, but it had been a home for a family over the centuries and its very timelessness lent a strength through to comfort. Ann felt she could learn to accept the place as her home and to feel safe. To feel safe, at that moment, was of more importance to her than to feel loved or wanted. Anyway, Opal wanted her. 'It's going to happen, this marriage, Tom, because of Opal. He wants me, for some reason, to have charge of Opal. I don't think Minerva will be able to do much, because it's clear she doesn't want to take good charge of Opal, and Opal doesn't like her.'

'But I get the feeling she wants to be Mrs Howard Crayne,' Tom said soberly, 'and from what she said, I get the feeling that that chap's mother also wants her to be the daughter-in-law. Certainly she doesn't want you, lass. And I don't want to feel that you're unwanted anywhere.'

In a way, Ann was sorry to have to say goodbye to Tom, even though he had firmly said he had cancelled his hotel booking in St Ives and had decided to stay in Regent's Bay, in a nice little pub called The Spanish Galleon. She watched his big rangy figure loping away; a young man who would cherish the woman he loved, and make neat and happy the little home he would provide. He would be proud of his children; he would take the boys to the park on Sunday and teach them how to kick a football, and he would help the girls with their home-work, and be proud of their good looks as they grew up. But Ann recalled the way he had looked at Felicity each time he had seen her. She, for some reason, was his ideal woman, which surprised Ann, for Tom was a sensible young man and should have known very well that Felicity couldn't cook or do practical things and didn't want to learn. Unless Felicity had let him think she did the cooking? But no, he had dropped in too often to the flat and found Ann at the stove. No, it was Felicity's charm and glamour he was chasing, like some bright rainbow that hid where it ended.

But it helped to know that he was only in

the village, a willing ear to listen to her problems, a real friend. She walked unseeingly through the grounds after he had left her. The light was draining out of the sky when she finally forced herself to go into the house. She must return now. She supposed that she and the child would have to attend the evening meal. She wondered what it would be like, now that it was known that she had lied over being jilted. Howard's mother would have been told, and Minerva would have other things to add. Ann was puzzled as to how Howard thought they could go on, while Minerva was staying in the house. She had heard Mrs Farraker mutter that now Minerva was in, she would be hard to be dislodged. It appeared that although Minerva was rich she had not yet acquired a home of her own. Just before his death her husband had sold the town house that Minerva had disliked so much and was in process of buying another one, in a smarter street. The country house had also been sold because of lack of staff, and Minerva had been trying to persuade her late husband to buy a villa in the south of France because she hated the English winters. No, she would stay here until the bitter end, Ann supposed.

But that was so soon, she thought, with a little gasp of surprise. Time was fleeting. The date that Howard had fixed was hardly a week away now, and she had so far made little effort to think about it or to prepare. It was something she had not wanted to think about, once it had penetrated her head what he had planned and that there was no real way of getting out of it, without being without a roof over her head again.

She wished she could peep into the future, see how it would work out. She entered the house by a little back door and worked her way up through the back staircases, unwilling to run into Howard or Minerva before she really must. And so she missed a great deal of excitement and telephoning. Knowing there must have been a fuss with Opal over getting cleaned, she was intent only on reaching the child and trying to talk her into a good mood before the evening meal.

It was when she reached their floor that the trouble burst upon her. Mrs Farraker was coming out of their suite as if she had been looking for Ann. 'Oh, where have you been, ma'am?' she asked, and the last word made Ann look sharply at her. Something must be very wrong for her to speak like that.

'Out for a walk,' Ann said. 'Why? What has happened?'

'Oh, the most terrible thing. The master is beside himself. Didn't you hear all the fuss downstairs?'

'I came up the back stairs. Tell me, Mrs Farraker, what is it? Is his mother ill?'

'No, it's the child!' Mrs Farraker said, her jaw dropping.

Ann pushed past her and went into their rooms. 'She isn't there,' the housekeeper said. 'Like I'm trying to tell you – she somehow heard that you weren't staying, so she ran away!'

'Ran away? Where? When?' Ann asked in bewilderment, and the thought crossed her mind that Minerva might have told the child that Ann was going away with Tom Westbury.

Mrs Farraker hesitated. 'The child says she hears voices in the air.'

'Oh, I know – I take no notice of that,' Ann said impatiently. When–'

'You should, miss,' Mrs Farraker said, slipping back in her manner. Now she was too worried to care how she spoke. 'That child gets the right stories even though she dresses 'em up with frills of her own. Like I'm trying to tell you, she heard you and Mr Crayne having a row and you saying you were going, and she was like a little mad thing. I couldn't hold her or reason with her. She ran out of that door and I heard her footsteps going – you know how quick she is. I couldn't catch her and when I got down the stairs, there was no sign of her, but the door was wide open.'

166

'The front door? But Opal doesn't ever go out that way! We always use the lobby door.'

'You won't understand, will you, miss? She's gone!'

'Rot, Mrs Farraker. She's playing a trick on you. She probably left the big door open and went to hide, just to see everyone get excited looking for her.'

'Well, I must admit there's been a fine frenzy of searching since you went out. All those hours ago. But she isn't in the house. Every room has been searched – even the attics and the cellars.' She caught the gleam in Ann's eyes, and said rather grimly, 'Yes, and the place where my son has got all his animals and now they'll have to go, by order of the master. And you knew about it, didn't you?'

'And so did you, didn't you?' Ann said softly. 'But I tell you, she must be here somewhere. There isn't anywhere for her to go. Besides, she'd want to see me first, when I came back, to hear it from my own lips–'

'She did, didn't she? And Mrs Thornton clinched things by saying that she heard that it was a Mr Tom Westbury that you were going away with!'

'Minerva! Ah, yes, it would be her doing the damage!' Ann sounded so angry that the housekeeper was surprised. 'And when did the child go?'

When the housekeeper pinpointed the

167

actual time, Ann gasped. 'But that was hours ago! I must go and find her!'

'The master has people scouring the district in cars and on horseback, miss, and it's no use your going on foot because dark is falling already and the moor is no place for someone who's a stranger to it–' but Ann had already snatched up a thick jersey and slid her feet into heavier shoes, and ran past. 'Miss, don't go – the master will never forgive me.'

'If he's out searching too, how can he know?' Ann flung over her shoulder.

'Opal left a note, miss,' the frantic housekeeper thought to call out, and that brought Ann back. 'I forgot. Here it is, just as I found it propped up on the mantelpiece.'

It was so uncharacteristic of Opal, that Ann almost burst into tears as she read it. 'YOU NONE OF YOU UNDERSTAND DO YOU? IF ANN'S NOT STAYING THEN I'M NOT. SHE'S THE ONLY ONE I LIKE. DON'T LOOK FOR ME. I HATE YOU ALL!'

She stuffed the note in her pocket and went soberly downstairs. The men were returning for lanterns. She mingled with them. In her dark sweater and her dark trousers, her slender form looked rather boyish. She slipped out before the housekeeper obeyed Howard's whiplash voice to turn on lights everywhere, and the hall

168

sprang to unaccustomed brilliance, lighting all the faces of the motley collection of searchers – staff, villagers, people Ann recognised and strangers that she didn't. Someone in the Crayne household was lost on the moor so Regent's Bay turned out regardless, as they would have for one of their own who might be missing. Rain began to fall and the sea made threatening noises like the boom of distant thunder. Ann, the town girl, didn't know the noises a rough night in Cornwall could produce. All she could think of was a skinny child with glasses, and a history she kept to herself, but with deep-seated loneliness in her eyes sometimes that helped Ann to guess a little at what the first years of Opal's life had been like.

Where would she go? Ann tried the barns and outhouses of nearby farms and cottages, but the owners assured her that they had already searched. The search must have been going on all the time that she and Tom were walking over the cliffs discussing her own future. How could she have been so selfish and uncaring? She might have known that Opal would find out what had happened somehow and put her own construction on it, inevitably arriving at the wrong con- clusion. But to think that the child had now declared openly that Ann was the only one she wanted to be with! It produced a lump in

Ann's throat that wouldn't let her swallow, and she pressed on, without a lantern, unheeding now heavy slashing rain that advanced and retreated with each gust of wind, so that now she was being soaked, now she thought the rain had stopped, only to find it was a trick of the wind, and a Cornish storm had taken possession of the landscape. She also found she was alone in darkness.

NINE

Felicity peered through that same mist and said irritably to Tania, who was driving the car, 'You said you knew the county! What are we crawling like this for?'

Tania said sweetly, 'Because it's my car, duckie, and I don't want to finish up in a dyke. I think we'll call it a day. There are lights ahead. It looks like one of those jolly little hostelries that always have a room or two empty. And I'm very hungry, not to say thirsty.'

'It looks a seedy place to me. Besides, according to the map we should be near this place that that wretched Ann went to work at.'

'I thought you liked your cousin,' Tania said, raising her thin eyebrows, and raking Felicity's sultry lovely face with eyes that were shrewd and weary.

'Oh, so I do, but you know how it is! I should have telephoned her, I suppose, but I wanted to surprise her.'

'So you said,' Tania murmured dryly, and gave her attention to coaxing the car towards the rather awkward entrance to the pub's yard where other cars were parked.

It was the Crayne Arms, the better inn of the two in Regent's Bay. As Tania had shrewdly assessed, they had a spare room and plenty of good food, warmth and drink. The two girls were settled in and Tania was pleased. Her car had been taken good care of.

Felicity half listened to the talk going on in the bar. She was bored. The tie-up between the two girls hadn't been a success. She wanted Ann back again. They had been comfortable, she and Ann, because Ann had the quality of making people comfortable. Tania was prepared to have Ann join them, not only to take charge of the domestic running of their flat but also to pour oil on the almost daily troubled waters. It was having Ann back, or some other girl to share the flat with her. Felicity unadulterated was too much already.

The door had been left open for the landlord's wife to return with the pudding and more of their good ale. Suddenly the outer door crashed open and a big young man filled the space. Moisture dripped from his wild hair that was curling with the damp from the mist. Both girls looked at him with interest. He had a thick high-necked sweater on and a waterproof jacket and carried a blackthorn stick, but it was his handsome face and his air of importance that caught the imagination of both of them.

The landlord came out from behind the bar, and the young man said sharply, 'I want help, Will.' The voices rose again, drowning what he said next. '...she went out to help look for the child and I didn't know. I wouldn't have permitted it. She doesn't know the moor!'

He was clearly very upset, and so was everyone else. Felicity watched with fascinated eyes as every man drinking there either finished his tankard or put it down, and followed the young man out into the mist.

'Who is he?' Tania asked the landlord's wife.

'That's Mr Crayne from Kingsbride,' she said. ''Tis his young lady what he's going to marry, lost on the moor. Mighty treacherous, bogs and dykes and such. It's that child that started it. Where there's trouble, there's always that child ... and yet Miss Ann dotes on her and can do anything with her. Well, of course, she would run out if the child was lost...'

'Ann, did you say?' Felicity asked sharply. 'What's she got to do with it?'

'She's going to marry Mr Crayne,' Will's wife said slowly, not understanding how these strangers knew the folk at Kingsbride and hadn't gone straight there.

'Marry? But she's only been here a few weeks!' She made an impatient movement. 'She's my cousin. We were going to Kings-

173

bride but we thought it better to stop here till the mist cleared.'

That was different. Any cousin of Ann's was welcome here, Tania saw. She and Felicity got all the information they could, and talked it over when they were alone again. Tania smiled twistedly and held out her hand. 'My fiver,' she said, as Felicity looked surprised. 'Well, you've lost, haven't you? Or are you going to conveniently forget you bet me that Ann would come running back the minute she heard you needed her? Got herself snugly dug in down here, it seems, and going to marry that gorgeous man we saw just now.'

Felicity glowered. 'Okay,' she shrugged, and paid up. 'But I want it back again if it's all a mistake. Personally, knowing Ann, I don't see how such a thing could have happened. Men don't even *see* her. You know that.'

'Perhaps he lost his cook and Ann took over below stairs. That way is a surefire winner for her. You've told her so, often enough, you know you have!'

'Well, we'll see. I'm not usually wrong,' Felicity said in her surliest tone. The rest of the evening was devoted to pumping people to find out what had been going on. But this was the wrong place to gossip. These people were tenants of the Crayne family, and although they didn't like Howard's mother,

174

they liked him, and they adored Ann and her way with the child and with Jago. Jago wasn't mentioned. They all knew and protected Maud Farraker, and these were strangers.

And so, after sleeping the night through, and eating a hearty breakfast, the two girls left the inn for Kingsbride not knowing what had happened in the hours of darkness, when Howard had found Ann by sheer accident, almost drowning in a dyke, and thought he had lost her.

Mrs Farraker and Gertrude were both skilled at home nursing. They were both afraid, for perhaps the first time, after a moorland mist rescue. It was no new thing in these parts. Jago had once fallen in a dyke but he was so big and strong, he had got himself out, although he had been ten years younger than he was now, and he had got the cow he had been searching for, too. Jago had been out tonight, half crazy, helping search for Ann, terrified that he had lost his champion. His dogs were to be taken from him, it had been intimated. Also his birds. He needed Ann to protect him from the master, whose anger had burned from the eyes in that haughty face. Poor Jago hadn't the wit to understand that Howard Crayne had just realised that life would be bleak indeed if Ann didn't recover. He was in no mood to look kindly at the big young man that Minerva kept warning him about.

Minerva hadn't said much up till now. Dinner was served and they sat with the length of the long table between them. Howard was almost unaware of Minerva's presence, but Minerva liked the situation well enough. This is how they would sit if she could manage to oust that little pest Ann who had worked her way somehow into Howard's affections or schemes, to the extent of his proposing marriage. Marriage by arrangement it might be, but Minerva didn't trust any other woman. She was quite sure that Ann could make Howard become fascinated with her if only because she was so different from the sort of girls Howard had always known.

'You must eat,' she murmured, as Howard looked as if he were going to leave his food and jump up to investigate what was going on upstairs. The doctor had not long arrived, and there was much coming and going. Minerva could have told him, though she hadn't any nursing experience herself, that this was merely because Kingsbride was old and inconvenient, and everything for home nursing had to be carried upstairs and down. Kingsbride would either be modernised or sold, when she at last, with the help of his mother, ousted that pallid Ann and became Howard's wife. It was as bad, she told herself with wry humour, as in days gone by, when the females of this county had dreamed of becoming the Crayne bride. She was using the same weapons as they had; guile, smooth talking, consummate acting, watching him all the time. Trying to find a chink in his armour, as those brides of long ago had tried to pierce the armour of long dead arrogant Craynes, find a way to the heart if only by stealth and cunning.

'Where was the child found, by the way?' she asked him, thereby forcing him to resume his seat in sheer surprise.

'I have no idea. I haven't asked. Why?' he answered.

She was taken aback at his tone, and the quick temper rose in her that she was usually at such pains to hide from him. 'Howard, dear, this is me – Minerva! Not some tiresome stranger! Smile, don't look at me as if you hated me!'

They were alone now. The two girls who had served their meal had departed. He wondered briefly if they were risking finding their way home to the village in this thick mist or whether Mrs Farraker had kept them at Kingsbride for the night. Times had changed. The family no longer dressed for dinner and often served themselves from a chafing dish on the sideboard. Minerva, watching him narrowly, was also irritated by these new ways and was deciding to change all that when she married him. Servants were to be had, if there were money enough. With her fortune from her late husband, and the money Howard would inherit for marrying and taking care of that tiresome little brat with the impossible name ... *Opal...*

Her vagrant thoughts brought her to a startled halt. If that child ran away again and didn't get found next time, there would be no point in Minerva herself dreaming of the future. If he wasn't forced to, Howard wouldn't marry anyone. He was a born bachelor. She was worldly wise enough to realise that. 'Someone must know where she went and how she got out,' she murmured. 'It really ought to be gone into, to see she doesn't escape again.'

Alarm shot through Howard at such a thought. Opal's running away meant danger for Ann. He got to his feet. 'You're right,' he said abstractedly. 'I'll go at once and find out. You stay here, finish your food. Please!'

Before his tone, she stayed. He had been so preoccupied with Ann's condition that he hadn't even asked about the child. It had been enough that someone had found her. Minerva fretted about it. Would he be told the truth? She decided to slip out and go up the back stairs to the child's room, find out for herself.

Opal's bed was turned down, but no sign of the child herself. Minerva frowned but hearing subdued voices in the next room – Ann's – she tiptoed across to the door and opened it a crack. Mrs Farraker and Gertrude were leaving because Howard had entered the room.

Minerva felt chilled inside. Did nobody know or care where that child had been because of Howard's preoccupation over Ann's condition? Had they all forgotten? Or had she been sent to another room, because of Ann? That must be it.

Howard leaned over Ann. Minerva saw his hand flutter above her head as if to stroke it, then Ann moved. Her eyes, in the subdued light, were dark pools that he couldn't drag his gaze from.

'Ann!' Minerva had never imagined he could speak like that to any woman. Rage boiled up in her.

Howard was so unaccustomed to being tender, that all his anxiety suddenly spilled over, and in a roughened voice he said, 'What the devil did you mean by going out into a night like this, you a stranger on the moor? I forbade you to go out! You disobeyed me! Why?'

Ann said, in a husky whisper, 'Opal. How is she? Where did they find her?'

He didn't immediately answer, but when Ann began to struggle up, he pushed her back and said brusquely, 'Don't talk to me about that child! She has nine lives! She might have cost you yours! Now go to sleep, and I'll talk to you in the morning.'

Ann took it that Opal was in her room, safe and sound, so after a hesitant moment, she lay back and her eyes closed. Howard leaned over her, and to the watching Minerva, it seemed that his mouth brushed Ann's forehead, before he turned and left the room.

Minerva closed the door, and turned to leave. The child was standing watching her. Dirty, dishevelled, her glasses starred, as if they had fallen off and been trodden on. Mud was on her feet, but in her eyes was an accusing glare. 'You were listening at the door,' Opal said in a hushed voice filled with dislike.

Minerva raised her hand. For a moment, their loathing for each other was so deep that no sound came from either. Minerva only knew she wanted to strike that hating little face. Then, as the child realised what she intended and opened her mouth to yell, Minerva hissed, 'Quiet! Not a sound! Ann is very ill. Out – I want to do something about you!' and she put a hand on Opal's shoulder and propelled her from the room.

Opal thought it was bath and bed, with rough unloving hands, but Minerva propelled her down the main staircase to where

Howard had gone. Into the great dining-room, where he was standing brooding with his back to the fire. He had forgotten Opal again, she saw. He was filled with anxiety and wretchedness about Ann. The servants, he was thinking, would have done something about the child. Ann had somehow bewitched him so that he didn't direct his thoughts to where his duty lay.

Minerva said icily, 'I imagine you had dismissed this … from your mind. It was I who found her. Look at her! Ask her where she's been!'

Howard looked at Opal in horror. Opal was on firmer ground now. She had done battle daily with Howard, whenever he was at home, since she had first met him. In her young mind that had amounted to the one day in each of the nineteen weeks she had had to rub shoulders with him, and so far she had won. He just didn't know how to handle children and he didn't like to be made to appear a fool. She stood with her legs wide apart and glared up at him through splintered lens and waited.

Howard was badly shaken. If Ann ever found out he had merely presumed Opal to have been found, and not made sure, just because she herself had nearly died, she would never forgive him, he knew. He looked down at Opal with distaste. Was this really the child of Elaine, beautiful, beautiful Elaine, who could charm a man until his heart ached, and still keep him at arm's length? But of course, Opal probably took after Clive's family. He remembered things that had been whispered, and a shudder ran through him.

He said, 'Minerva, you mean well, but will you sit down and finish your food? Opal, have you eaten recently?'

The child shook her head. 'Do you want any food, Opal?' he persisted, but she set her mouth obstinately,. She was starving, but she wanted to get up to her room and peep in at Ann. From where she had been, she had heard things said, scaring things, that made her feel that her absence had some-how, in some queer way, almost resulted in Ann's not being there any more.

Minerva said, her voice rising, 'Are you dismissing me, Howard? Are you going to be *kind* to this … this tiresome child,' she said, forcing herself to temper her language, 'when she has caused all this trouble?'

He nodded abstractedly. 'I can remember how it looked when I was down at that height. I can remember how I felt, when adults all talked together and ignored me. Besides, to be dirty and cold and tired is not funny.'

He moved to the bell rope. Mrs Farraker came, and he said, quietly, 'Help Opal to have a nice warm bath and see there's a hot bottle in her bed.'

Mrs Farraker's mouth dropped open at the sight of her. Howard said, 'No unkindness, if you please. I'll talk to the child myself in the morning. How is Ann?'

'Asleep, sir,' Mrs Farraker said, shutting her mouth tightly. In the ordinary way there would have been high loud words between her and Opal, but of course they must all keep quiet. Just for tonight. Opal allowed herself to be led away.

'I don't understand you!' Minerva exploded, when they were alone.

Howard looked at her with great interest, down the length of the table. 'Would you like some more wine? No? Then tell me what you would have done, that I didn't do.' It was said so softly, she almost fell into the trap, exploding that she would have given the child a good beating, shaken her until she had disclosed where she had been, to cause all that fuss and trouble. But she kept such control of her angry tongue that it almost hurt her. At last, she shook her head and said, helplessly, 'I don't know. What you did, I suppose. Put her in the housekeeper's care, get her cleaned up and to bed. Talk it out tomorrow. It's just that I couldn't bear you to be so upset about one thing and another.'

'No, well...' He tried to concentrate on Minerva, to play the perfect host because

183

this was a guest of his mother's. But all he could see was that child and he didn't know what he was going to do with her, but do something he must, because of what she meant to Ann. Ann, who was beginning to colour his life, although they couldn't meet and exchange a few words without clashing. 'Minerva, how long are you intending to stay here?' he heard himself ask her, suddenly.

She looked outraged as he expected her to look. He didn't know why he'd said it. Suddenly he wanted the house to himself. To think, plan, sort out his own complicated emotions. His mother would be no problem to him; she had retired with one of her sulks, which she liked to call 'her migraine'. Gertrude was in attendance. He said to Minerva, 'I just wondered. I haven't heard what plans you intend to make. Oh, I'm trying to be the good host, when all the time ... Minerva, you must excuse me. I have things on my mind. No, I want no food. I must think ... about that child.'

'But I could help you...!' Minerva began, but he brushed the suggestion aside. 'My dear Minerva, if I don't know what to do with my own relative, I am quite sure you will not be able to.'

He had to talk to Opal in the morning, but all he wanted to do in the morning was to go in to see Ann. There were things to be said to her, things sharpened last night, in all its anxiety and pain.

In the end he got neither of those visits done because visitors called for Ann. He at once thought it was Tom Westbury and found he was one of the party. The others were two young women he had half distractedly noticed as strangers in the Crayne Arms last night, while he waited for helpers.

Felicity, deeply angry to think that Ann had fallen into such a cosy nest, buried her ire and managed to look very striking, in a new green and white striped dress and scarf tied round her hair. She was a complete foil for the vivacious Tania, who had elected to wear dead white with terrific effect. It was a golden sunny day, with sea mist slowly receding, leaving a haze over everything, which made one tend to forget the vicious elements of the night before. Felicity smiled alluringly and was quite confident that she would be shown up to Ann at once. Everyone in the pub had been talking about the rescue and of how Mr Crayne had been 'near out of his mind' to get Miss Ann back, but that the doctor had assured the neighbourhood that she was on the road to recovery. To think that Ann could already have dug herself in, with such popularity, was galling.

Galling, too, to find that Howard Crayne was not pleased to see the visitors. He came into the salon where they were waiting, looking with hostility at the good-humoured but anxious Tom Westbury, and then blightingly at the two girls. Which, he was asking himself, was the one who was the cousin, the one who had served Ann such a shabby trick so that she had had to hastily find a roof over her head, with a new job, a roof and job that might have been considerably less safe than this one. He looked at them both, and unerringly picked Felicity. Yes, that would be the one.

He wasn't going to let them see Ann, but the Quarleys arrived, which rather messed things up. The Quarleys had met Ann the once, and had liked her. They didn't like Minerva. Sir Victor didn't expect to be allowed in the sick-room, but his wife did. Howard perversely let her go up first. The housekeeper had orders to restrict visitors to a few minutes.

Lady Quarley settled comfortably by Ann's bed. 'I have tried to visit you since the engagement party, dear,' she began, with her comfortable smile, 'but we seem to have been stopped somehow. I don't think they want you to have local visitors somehow. But when I heard what had happened, I said to Sir Victor, "It's no use, I am going to see that poor girl." What a nasty experience, dear. Everyone's talking about it! How are you feeling?'

Ann smiled. 'I'm much better, thanks, but it was so unexpected. Tell me, have you seen little Opal this morning? They won't let me have any news about her. She *is* all right, isn't she?'

Lady Quarley said, 'She got her glasses broken, the housekeeper told me. But it seems she's having new ones, but she's a bit sorry for herself at the moment. But don't worry about her. She's around, up and dressed.'

Ann's relief was the hurting kind. Lady Quarley, chased from the sick-room, told her husband, as he drove them home, that they must try and persuade the Craynes to let Ann and the child come on the boat for a week-end.

'Not much hope of that!' Sir Victor grumbled. 'It was made very plain that the little bride-to-be wasn't going anywhere, but I've got stuck with those two girls and the young fellow. Crayne doesn't want them around, I suppose.'

'Oh, neither do I!' Lady Quarley said, indignantly. 'I didn't like them at all, least of all the one who said she was that nice Ann's cousin.'

'Yes, well, there's something funny going on there, seems to me!'

Tom could have told them what it was

about. He went to see Ann with the girls, because it was as natural as breathing to make such a visit. But the minute he was inside Kingsbride, he knew he had done the wrong thing. Howard left them with Minerva to play hostess, and Minerva managed to split them up so that she had Tom to herself. She showed him the conservatories while the girls were left free to 'go upstairs and see dear Ann'. Tom didn't like Minerva because he loathed women with so much make-up on. True, hers suited her but it made him nervous. She was different from Felicity and Tania. They had gaiety and youth and fun to help out their glossy appearance, but Minerva had a kind of way with her that made Tom afraid to speak for fear she used what he said.

Gently pumping him, with all the time in the world, because the girls wouldn't be allowed near Ann, and Howard was at last having his little talk with Opal, Minerva found out what the set-up was and why Ann had come to Kingsbride. Now Minerva could see much more clearly what Howard was trying to do. But there were so many gaps. She was sure that Howard's mother knew a great deal more but although she was scheming for Minerva to have Howard, she wouldn't disclose just what she did know. So Minerva did the next best thing and worked on Tom.

'She's very unhappy, you know,' she murmured. 'She's only going into this marriage because of the child. Very fond of children, dear Ann is.'

Tom knew that. He could have added that Ann adored everyone who needed her, especially animals. But he just let Minerva talk.

'I don't know all the details, of course,' she mused, 'but if I were you I wouldn't go too far away. She'll need you, poor Ann, pretty soon ... unless of course I've made an awful mistake and it's the pretty Felicity you're keen on. Oh, do say I haven't messed everything up!'

Tom assured her very quickly that it wasn't Felicity at all. He had been dazzled by her at first, but it was Ann he was keen on now, and he was staying there another week at least before he went to Scotland to take up his new job.

Minerva pumped him about it and told him that that was what Ann secretly wanted. Her own small house near her husband's new job, not a great house like Kingsbride and a cold man like Howard Crayne, nor a ready-made family, much as she adored children. She was clever and didn't make her argument too obvious, but managed to make Tom feel he had been rather blind in the past, and that Ann had liked him too much for too long.

Howard could see Minerva walking Tom in the grounds, and was pleased that she was keeping him away from Ann while he talked with Opal.

The child went into a mulish mood at once, so he sat down and beckoned to her. 'I'm not going to punish you. I just wanted to know why you wanted to run away from Kingsbride and Ann, who I thought you rather liked.'

Opal kept her mouth tight shut. She knew grown-ups only too well. Just one confiding remark and you were asked another leading question and yet another. So she decided to say nothing.

'Perhaps I was mistaken,' Howard went on gently. 'Perhaps you don't like Ann after all.' But the swift upward searching look from the child's eyes behind those splintered glasses was enough to say she did care about Ann. 'So why did you run away?'

He wasn't a patient man and although he tried, he had never been able to make much contact with Opal. He said, 'Well, if you won't tell me why you ran away, at least tell me where you got to! Heavens, I don't even know who found you nor when!'

'I came back!' Opal muttered at last.

'Did you know that Ann nearly drowned, looking for you in the mist?'

Opal hung her head. She knew all about what had happened. She had cried herself sick in the night, terrified that Ann might have died. The rest of the time she spent hating Minerva, who pried and spoiled everything. She looked up hopefully at Howard. Dare she tell him about Minerva? But instinct shrieked in her tired brain to keep quiet, so she merely nodded, signifying that she did know how nearly Ann's life had been snuffed out, due to her own badness. One slow tear ran down her cheek, but she bit hard on her lips and wouldn't let herself cry. Her self-restraint was more embarrassing to Howard than if she had been a natural eleven-year-old and stood and bawled. He got up and said, 'Well, don't run away again and do try and behave!' in his old sharp voice and left her. And he didn't know that she had been almost on the point of weakening and telling him what she knew about Minerva.

He gave orders that Opal's new glasses must be fetched, and that she must be kept in her room. But he forgot that her room was next to Ann's, and that she found a moment to creep in, when everyone had gone down and left Ann to sleep.

Opal was scared because Ann looked so white and thin and ill. 'What happened to you?' she squeaked. 'It was only last night!'

'Had a rough time in the mist, sweetie,' Ann said, hugging the child to her. 'What happened to you? Don't you know I couldn't go on if you'd been lost on the moor?'

Opal sobbed unrestrainedly with Ann. She cried so hard that when she was finished, she fell asleep and so didn't get round to telling Ann where she'd been. When Howard looked in again later, he found them both asleep, cuddled so tightly together that he felt sharply unhappy, curiously shut out. On the table by the bedside were some wild flowers that Jago had picked and made his mother promise to put in a little pot to give Ann. Already they were wilting. Howard's hot-house blooms he had sent, had been relegated to a corner table, as of no importance. The little cat had crept in unobserved and was cuddled up in one of the small armchairs and was trying hard to remain unseen, and two fat paws were visible under the bed, and a puppy's nose and one black eye peeped out and shot back again. Howard resisted the temptation to turn the animals out. It would create havoc up here, when at the moment all seemed so peaceful. But he must really speak to the housekeeper about it.

He let himself out of the room and softly closed the door. The doctor had assured him that the wedding, fixed for the end of the week, could go forward, as it was to be such a quiet affair.

The end of the week. Not many days

ahead now, because Ann would be, at least in name and in law, his wife, to protect. But as he went down the main staircase, he couldn't rid himself of the feeling that at the end of the week that desirable circumstance would not take place.

TEN

'Is this the brat you're supposed to be looking after?' Felicity drawled, in a soft voice which suggested she thought Opal, sitting near the window with a book held in front of her, would neither hear nor understand.

Ann was so distressed. 'Oh, hush, Felicity, she'll hear! Yes, that's Opal, and she is very sweet!'

Felicity made a soft derisory noise with her soft carefully made-up mouth, which Opal saw, without moving her head. She now had her new glasses. It was good to be able to see without feeling one's eyes were being strained, but she had plenty of other troubles to take the place of breaking the old ones. Howard was seeing too much of that Minerva and Opal had heard them discussing the wedding as if it were Minerva's, not Ann's. Opal didn't know much about who arranged for what, at weddings, but she had ample scope to hear what everyone else was saying. The kitchen staff were incensed because Ann was being sent to her room like an invalid until the actual wedding day. Howard's mother was furious because Howard was still intending to marry Ann and not to postpone it, as she had persuaded the doctor to arrange. Minerva was not, it appeared, doing very much to alter the situation, Mrs Crayne considered, and Gertrude was uneasily teetering between one party and another, watched by the child, who felt by instinct that Gertrude, who had been so promising at the start, was now nobody's friend.

And now Felicity was here, and another potential enemy, Opal thought. Felicity said, 'I can't think how you managed to catch that handsome man!' and ignored Ann's frown.

Ann turned in desperation to the child. 'Opal, dear, I'm sure you can't manage to study with our voices going. Take your map book into the schoolroom and write me an imaginary journey from – look, let me show you. From here to … let me see, there! Yes, that should be very interesting. Try your best!'

Opal said, standing on one foot at the side of the bed, 'I can't go. Uncle Howard said I was to stay with you. All the time.'

'Did he indeed!' Ann's brows shot up. Any suggestion of Howard's being bossy still had entirely the wrong effect on her. 'Then in that case, off you go! Whatever next!' and she gently pushed the child towards the door.

'Now,' she said to Felicity, when they were

alone, 'What are you doing down in this part of the world, and how could you be so clumsy as to say those things in front of the child?'

Felicity shrugged and grinned. 'Just wanted to see how you'd rise to the bait. Well, you must admit, it looks very queer, your snaffling a rich handsome man but having such a hole-and-corner little marriage. Well, it *is*, isn't it?'

Ann's pale face flushed. She was still feeling far from well, though drugs had effectively warded off the chill she might have caught, after that night in the dyke. She lay back and regarded Felicity. 'Why did you come?'

'We were touring. Well, word came that dear Tom had come down here, with your trunk. I suppose you asked him to bring it. Then a fishy story was being banded around about you having said you'd been jilted by him, just to get this job. Now, do explain, darling, how you of all people, could have been so bright as to cook up a yarn like that?'

'I didn't ask Tom to bring the trunk. I wrote to Mrs Tate to ask her to send it on, as I'd arranged. I've nothing to say about my marriage to Howard Crayne, and now you've visited me, I think you'd better go! Please!'

Felicity didn't make any move to go. 'Oh,

don't be like that, Ann. Sorry and all that, but you know me. Speak first, think afterwards.'

Ann ignored that blatant stretching of the truth. Felicity rarely said a thing before she had thoroughly considered its worth as a sting or a cajoling remark, depending on what she hoped to get as the outcome of the conversation. She said instead, 'I'm surprised Tania didn't come with you.'

For some reason, Felicity didn't like that. She said, 'Tania is being rather beastly at the moment and taken herself off, angling for some frightful little man just because it's rumoured he's got some cash. Thank heavens I don't have to chase a man!'

That was so true that Ann didn't question it. She said, 'Poor Tom was so much in love with you. Did you have to hurt him the way you did?'

Felicity watched her through veiled lids. Ann was transparent, or she seemed so. But now, Felicity reminded herself, it appeared that Ann had quietly got herself a rich husband, and still managed to look as if she didn't know how it had come about. 'I didn't hurt him. I think you hurt him, though. The way you got yourself this husband all in a hurry. Tom can't believe it!'

'That isn't anyone else's business,' Ann said quietly, with a new implacability that Felicity hadn't known was there.

Felicity stayed as long as she dare, and in that time she told Ann about how nice Howard was to all his guests, and wondered innocently just what part Minerva played in the outfit, and what would happen about Opal in the future, and finished, 'I wouldn't like to take on a child that age. I mean, there must be something odd about the set-up. There has to be! It's this business about her not being sent away to school. Well, I gather there's a *reason* why she daren't be allowed among other girls. Any ideas on what that reason is?'

Ann's heart began to thud in the old way. Had she not lain awake at night worrying around this odd question, which nobody would explain. Surely, as the new wife, she should know about it? She would ask Howard outright. But he always eluded her questions, made her feel as if she were being unpardonably inquisitive. But she had her pride. She said coldly, 'But I know why she isn't to go away to school. And no, I'm not going to discuss it with anyone else. Now be a dear and go, Felicity, because I'm suddenly very tired.'

Felicity believed she had made her point better than she had intended. Ann was near tears. You had to work very hard to bring Ann to that point, Felicity knew well enough. She got up, shrugging as she bent and lightly kissed Ann's cheek. With a bit of luck, Ann would think twice about this marriage. She liked things to be 'out in the open', Felicity remembered. Felicity herself didn't care. She would have entered into any sort of marriage so long as there was big money for all the extravagances she craved. She told Ann she'd come again, and she sauntered downstairs to try and find Howard.

He was at the foot of the grand staircase, presumably just about to go up. Felicity feigned surprise at seeing him. 'Oh, I thought you were out somewhere!' she said, and looked very guilty. 'Oh, dear. Oh, well, I don't suppose it will matter. I mean, when you're marrying someone as a business proposition, I don't suppose you care what they do by way of amusement. Well, I mean – Ann isn't consciously being deceitful. Oh, dear, I'm making it worse, aren't I?'

'What is it that Ann is supposed to be doing? Isn't she still in bed?'

Felicity's eyes widened at his cold tone. 'Oh, now you're cross with me! Honestly, I wouldn't have taken Tom *into* her bedroom. At least, only if Ann had said so. I mean, to talk through an open door is respectable, isn't it, or don't you think so?'

Howard said, 'Are you telling me that Westbury is visiting Ann?'

Felicity pursed up her lips. 'I'm not saying anything because I think you would be very mean to Ann if you could. It's bad enough about that child, but there, everyone trespasses on Ann's good nature and she really doesn't think the things she does look wrong. It's just that she can't say "no".'

Minerva, with the salon door open a crack, was rather amused to find that Ann's cousin was very good at stirring up trouble by just hint or suggestion – here was the sort of person she had been hoping to meet for some time. She watched Howard storming upstairs to Ann's room, no doubt expecting to find Tom Westbury with her. What could have been better to help Minerva's own plans?

She watched Felicity ruefully study her nails for a moment, then she came softly out to where the girl stood. 'Don't expect Howard Crayne to succumb to anyone's charms, my dear, considerable though yours may be. He's a born woman-hater,' Minerva said, smiling maliciously as Felicity flushed darkly.

'Oh, I wasn't trying to make him–' Felicity began.

'Of course you weren't. Men are such fickle beasts, aren't they? There's that Tom Westbury of yours – he's just been telling me how he's madly in love with Ann. I wonder why men are so intrigued with these door-mattish girls? Come in the library. I want a little talk with you. You interest me.'

Felicity didn't like her, but she was so seething against the way Howard had looked, and the obvious fact that, as Minerva had hinted, he was cherishing a rising interest in Ann, that she followed. All her life she had calmly taken men who had started an interest in Ann, and she couldn't break the habit.

Minerva talked to her quite seriously, about the fact that the family had a secret, and that there was only one way to deal with it, but Howard wouldn't agree, and had taken up this mad idea of marrying Ann as a way out. 'He hasn't told her, of course, that he intends to annul the marriage within the year, because she'll be of no more use to him then. It's the terms of an old Will, you see. But his mother is furious. There were other ways of settling it, but he is so self-willed.' She talked for a long time, but she didn't disclose what the family secret was or how Ann would fit in after the marriage, which was obviously merely a ploy to bring about the transference of a great deal of property. Minerva hinted that Ann should be led to believe that Howard had no regard for her at all, because as Minerva finished up, 'She's very naïve and I think she is beginning to think that Howard is becoming interested in her. If only someone could make her see sense that that wasn't the case, without actually putting it in so many words, of course.'

Felicity didn't offer to do this little job, but she saw no reason why she should refuse Minerva's request to take up a tray to Ann. While with Ann, she could usefully tell her that Tom Westbury was still carrying a torch for Felicity herself, since Ann seemed to think he was such a nice young man. Felicity didn't want him but she saw no reason why he should be left hanging about here for Ann, if this marriage fell through, as Minerva seemed so passionately to want it to.

She pulled a face at the contents of the jug on the daintily laid tray. 'What is it? It smells awful!' she grimaced.

'My dear, it's only a tisane. For Ann's bad heads. It seems to do her good. No, I didn't make it – I'm not domesticated, I'm afraid. It's Howard's mother who brews such a fine tisane.'

'Will Ann drink it?'

'Don't sound so doubtful. Take it up to her. Well, tell her Howard sent it. She'll do it for him, you'll see.'

Howard had got nowhere with Ann. He had found her crying quietly but bitterly, and when he asked her what the matter was, she turned her back on him. Something had gone very wrong. His face was stony, and he looked very irritable at her tears. Opal was upset, and Gertrude hadn't been near Ann.

And why, she asked herself, was she being kept in bed? Useless to ask Howard, so she refused to answer him.

'I am told Westbury came up to visit you,' Howard said distinctly. 'Is that true?'

Ann caught the distaste in his voice, and swung over to look at him in indignation and astonishment. Her face was wet, blotched with tears, and her hair lay splayed over the pillow. Something about her, seeing her like this for the first time, made him feel odd, ill at ease. He wanted to gather her to him and tell her it would be all right after the wedding day, but he was so unemotional, so un-demonstrative, and so rattled already by the way things seemed to be going so wrong. His mother was hatching something with Minerva, he was sure, because Minerva was looking so suddenly smug. He wished she would take his advice and set about looking for a place of her own, but he could do nothing. She was a guest of his mother's, and he had to be very careful how he handled his mother. He loathed her moods and the feeling of intrigue in the house.

'If you don't know better than that, why ask me?' Ann gasped, her eyes hostile.

'Ann, I know this is only a marriage of convenience...' he began, but broke off sharply because the words had a hollow ring. It wasn't true any more.

Ann said sharply, 'Exactly. For Opal's

sake. Don't you ever forget that. It's Opal who counts, with me. Nobody else, nobody!'

There didn't seem to be anything else he could say to that. He got up and left her room, and went into the child's room. The corridor was empty and silent when Felicity came up a few minutes later with her tray.

Ann stared at it. 'What's that?' she asked wearily.

'Don't ask me,' Felicity said, 'and I don't think I like being treated as a housemaid. I was practically told to bring it up. I understand you like it.'

'Oh, tea,' Ann said, and drank it without much interest, pulling a face at the end because she said it had been over-sweetened.

'Well, I didn't do that,' Felicity assured her. 'I expect you want me to go, so I'll say goodbye. Shall I come again?' But at Ann's surprised look, she shivered again and said, 'Oh, no, well, perhaps not. Am I invited to this hole-and-corner wedding or not?' but Ann was unable to steady her voice enough to answer. Hole-and-corner wedding exactly described it at that moment. She lay staring hopelessly at the door long after Felicity had removed the tray and herself, and the sounds of her footsteps had died away.

Howard, in the child's room, was trying to

persuade Opal to talk. He wasn't very good with children, and something about Opal had always irritated him. He kept thinking of Elaine, and a new thing was bothering him. Up till quite recently he had tried to keep the memory of Elaine smothered in the background. It was too painful to take out and look at. But now Elaine's face and vivid personality had somehow got blotted out by Ann's face. He couldn't understand it, because Ann was a quiet person, not beautiful at all. Yet she had blotted Elaine out. He stared at Opal, wondering if this child, who was also unprepossessing, would flare into a vivid personality when she grew up. He leaned forward and gently removed the child's glasses.

'They're new,' Opal said fiercely. 'Ann chose the frames. Don't you like them?'

He stared at the child, not answering. Opal made her face go deadpan which was unfortunate at that moment. It was about as interesting as a lump of dough. Howard sighed and put the glasses back, saying idly, 'Very nice,' and thinking of Ann and wondering why he had come in here. But there had been a very cogent reason. He drew a deep breath and tried again.

'Look, for better or worse, you and I have got to accept the fact that we are stuck with each other until you're grown up.'

'And Ann, Ann, too?' Opal asked urgently,

205

so he nodded. 'And Ann, too.'

Opal breathed a sigh of relief. 'Then that's all right.' But on an afterthought, a rather unfortunate afterthought, Opal said, 'You won't let that Tom Westbury take her away? I mean, I like him. He's a good sort. I've not seen him much but he's known Ann for ages. Sort of cosy. But don't let him take her away.'

It ruined everything. Howard got up and said coldly, 'How can he, since Ann will be marrying me at the end of this week?' and he went out, into the empty and silent corridor, black thoughts jumbled up in his mind that bothered him very much, because there was no real reason why he should care one way or another, what friends had been Ann's before she came here.

Ann heard his footsteps go by the door. She had thought for a moment that he would return and then she would tell him she was sorry she had snapped at him, and to explain everything about Felicity and Tom and make it clear to him that she was prepared to do everything to smooth the way if only he would tell her the truth about this queer marriage. What was the secret of Opal's birth? To Ann, it seemed reasonable for her to know, and most unreasonable of Howard to continue like this.

She couldn't have said when she began to feel ill. Howard first knew of the panic on, when he returned from the stables. He had been inspecting the gift he had bought for Ann: a delicate little beauty of a mare which Minerva coveted. She had pointed out that as yet nobody knew if Ann rode. Howard couldn't remember if he had asked Ann or not. But she must learn to ride and she must be well mounted.

People were actually running about, at Kingsbride. The doctor's car shot up the drive. Mrs Farraker's face was chalk white and that son of hers following her about, like a hulking shadow, and every so often his big hand turned his mother round by the shoulder as if she were made of thistledown. 'She ain't going to die, is she?' he repeatedly demanded. 'Who tried to kill her then? Who?'

It was some time before Howard could get any sense out of anyone, except that Ann was suddenly so ill that even Mrs Crayne had ventured from her room.

It was a terrible day. Howard vetoed the idea of Ann being swept off to the county hospital. The journey would kill her, he said. Everything had to be procured for her in this house. Nobody could tell him what had happened. Nobody had seen Felicity go to Ann's room with a tray. Nothing was mentioned of that. Ann just started being violently sick and in terrible pain. Jago had found her in the corridor near the window, which was open, and the biting wind from the moors was sweeping in. Poor Jago did the only thing he could think of. He knew he mustn't go into Ann's room with her, so he picked her up like a puppy in his arms, cuddled to his great strength and warmth, and took her down the back stairs to his mother. It was the best thing he could have done. The staff quarters were cosy and warm. In the housekeeper's bedroom Ann was looked after like Mrs Farraker's own child. The doctor said Ann was to be kept there where she was, if possible.

'How was it nobody heard her call?' Howard demanded. Nobody could tell him. She had been left up there to rest, on his orders. He had said Opal was not to go in to her, so Opal had gone off on some secret pursuit of her own, nobody knew where, and Kingsbride didn't boast of anything so modern as a bell in any but the best bedrooms on the first floor.

Howard's mother didn't rave, as usual. Her presence below stairs, looking at Ann's now dead-white and still face, put the staff into a complete flutter. Minerva went down too, to visit, and the doctor and Howard seemed to dwarf the big arched kitchen to which they repaired afterwards for coffee and cakes. Howard recalled sharply his chill foreboding earlier, as he was now assured that Ann would live, but there would be no wedding at the end of the week. And nobody could say what had happened to upset her.

The wedding preparations went forward for the following week. It had a hollow feeling now. A small quiet wedding in a great house like this was all wrong, anyway. Standing by Ann's bed in the housekeeper's own room, Howard suddenly wanted to see Ann in white, with four little train bearers, and bridesmaids. But it was Elaine's big society wedding he was thinking of and he knew Ann wouldn't like that sort of thing. But would she, if they were like any other couple, *in love?* Those two words produced such an astonishing riot of emotions in him that he promised himself he wouldn't think of them any more. Instead, he went about his usual business in a fury of efficiency, and took on other business to eat into the hours and prevent him from thinking. There was a lot to do about the postponed wedding. Lawyers to be seen. There was the little mare that he had bought for Ann, and there was, moreover, the business of where that child kept disappearing to. Howard sent one of the girls from the village to stay with Opal all the time, but even then, the child escaped and even a threatened beating wouldn't make her disclose where she had been.

Ann was young and resilient and didn't like being below stairs. She was worried about Opal and when she was well enough she was returned to her room and had the child with her all day.

Three days before the new date for that unfortunate wedding, Felicity telephoned Ann. Ann was now up for the latter half of each day. Howard was extremely tiresome, she thought, in being so dictatorial. But as she felt at present, it was easier to do as he wished than to try to argue with him. He bought her expensive flowers and gifts. Boxes of wonderful clothes had been steadily arriving. Gertrude, muted now, but sending out unreadable messages from those hooded eyes of hers, attended Ann whenever Mrs Crayne didn't want her, but would answer no questions.

That morning, Howard looked in after Ann had slowly dressed and was sitting by the window. It was the sort of day to be out; cold but breezy and sunny. She wished she felt stronger.

Howard stood by her, looking down at her. 'Ann, I haven't asked you this before, but you've been very ill and nobody has an idea why or how. Do *you* know what made you ill?'

Ann could remember only the odd-tasting tea that Felicity had brought her that day, but she knew better than to say so. Howard had shown he hadn't approved of Ann having visitors of her own. Felicity suggested Tom Westbury to him. Tom had already run the risk of writing to her, sending her flowers; somehow he had persuaded Jago to get them into the house. Tom's easy friendliness and ordinary air would, of course, inspire confidence in poor Jago who thought he was doing what Ann would like. So Ann just shook her head.

'But it must have been something you ate that day, Ann. You must remember so that it can be eliminated from your diet. We want no recurrence of this after our marriage!'

He didn't know what he meant exactly himself, except that after the end of the week he meant to try to persuade Ann, once she was his wife, that life could be very good between them and that they might possibly make something of that marriage. But it was still such tender ground and Ann was so much inclined to fly into a temper and she had been so very ill, he had at one time almost felt she was slipping away from him, even though the doctor assured him that the worst was over. He sat down by her and took her hand in his but she didn't like the upset feeling she got, and snatched her hand away. 'I don't know, I don't know,' she repeated. 'All I can say is, I'll never drink tea again!'

She coloured. She had let it slip out. He pounced on it. 'Tea! What tea? Who brought it to you? How was it nobody knew of it? Who is keeping it from me?'

Ann waved a shaky hand. 'Oh, it was nothing. Probably the milk was a bit sour. I don't know. Felicity isn't very domesticated and wouldn't know, and anyway, it was a kind thing to do,' she said hastily, 'the kitchen staff being so overworked.' But the damage was done. Howard stormed and raged about Felicity, so Ann, in her cousin's defence, said, 'It couldn't possibly have been that, and anyway, why bother now? People often don't notice if the milk's gone off. Oh, do leave me in peace, Howard! You do make things so uneasy when you're around!'

She didn't understand why he looked so wounded. Quite suddenly he decided to go. He turned on his heel, and it struck her that the set of his shoulders wasn't as arrogant as usual. There was almost a dejected air about him.

And then Felicity telephoned. Ann went down to the corridor below, where there was a telephone in one of the guest rooms, and took the call. Felicity said breathlessly, 'I've just heard you've been ill. How? Well, from Tom, of course!'

That 'of course' did just what Felicity had intended it to do. Those two were back together again. Well, Felicity could twist any man round her little finger, couldn't she? Ann put it to the back of her mind and said, 'Well, I wanted to speak to you. The only thing I'd had that day which could have

212

upset me was the tea you brought up. Who asked you to bring it to me?'

'Now wait a bit. You don't think I did anything to make you ill, do you?'

'Oh, don't be silly,' Ann begged wearily. 'It's just that Howard keeps on questioning me because nobody seems to know what made me ill. I felt like death, I don't mind admitting. I never want to be sick like that again!'

'Well, it's nothing to do with me. That Mrs Thornton gave me the tray. She said it was a tisane, and you liked them because they were good for your headaches.'

'I don't have headaches!' Ann said indignantly. 'Minerva asked you to bring it to me?' Her heart thumped painfully.

Felicity said quickly, 'Yes, but she said it was Howard's mother who made it. She's always making tisanes, she said. What is it, a sort of herb tea? Ugh! What made you drink it if you didn't like the stuff?'

Ann couldn't remember and said so. 'And Howard isn't pleased because the wedding had to be postponed.'

'Well, I shouldn't worry. I expect it will go on being postponed. It seems your Howard is a lad who likes the girls and doesn't like the marriage tie,' Felicity said cheerfully.

'He isn't like that at all! What gave you that impression?' Ann protested.

'Now don't get all steamed up. He was just

213

being nice to me because I'm a sort of cousin of yours, I suppose. Although I did get the impression from Mrs Thornton that he likes girls with no strings attached. Anyway, I had no fault to find with his entertaining ... oh, I suppose I shouldn't have said that. Well, you know how the lads all seem to like me. Anyway, why should you care? You never did like ceremony, and that Kingsbride set-up hardly seems to be your scene, dear. Well, I mean, I gather Howard's wife will have to entertain all the big shots of the county and that Howard's mother doesn't think you ... oh, why don't I shut my big mouth? Well, you must admit that you'd be happier doing a bit of cooking or home nursing and not having to entertain people like Sir Victor Quarley and his family.'

'They're nice people,' Ann said. 'I quite like Lady Quarley. When did you meet them?'

Felicity bit her lip. She was sore at the Quarleys and hadn't known that Ann was getting on well with them. Tania had managed to get an invitation to the party on the Quarley yacht and was getting very friendly with the Quarleys' son's best friend, but Felicity hadn't been included in the invitation.

'Haven't you been invited to their parties yet? I thought you might have been. They're quite something,' Felicity said airily. 'I say, I

214

didn't mean to be so rotten about your wedding. You'd like me to come, wouldn't you?'

'It isn't what I'd like,' Ann said quietly. 'I didn't have the task of sending out the invitations. I'm afraid I have no say in it at all.'

'Well, don't worry,' Felicity said. 'I'll ask Howard tonight when he takes me – oh, dash, forget I said that. Look, I must rush,' and she rang off, leaving Ann with the sick conclusion that Howard, too, had fallen to Felicity's insidious charm like every other man, and that Tom, too, had gone back to her.

It was Howard's mother, apparently who took the 'hole-and-corner' feeling from the wedding. Ann couldn't decide whether it was family pride, or a feeling of malice that made that beautiful elderly woman set Ann in the middle of the county that day. Or that was how it seemed to Ann. A small wedding? The little church in Regent's Bay was packed to overflowing with important people, and the press, and police help had had to be invoked to settle the parking question. Ann, in a gown that was so starkly plain that it might have been openly labelled Paris, carried the curiously strong likeness of one of Howard's ancestresses. It was uncanny. Afterwards Ann was inclined to think that Gertrude, for reasons of her own, and knowing the old portraits so well, had deliberately chosen that gown, and her clever fingers had made Ann's long hair carry the suggestion of that other woman's in the 300-year-old portrait, without being actually a copy. The suggestion was eagerly lapped up by the fashion magazines and the newspapers. Ann, frozen with the strangeness of it all, and the new-found knowledge that every time she looked at Howard the memory of Felicity's suggestions as to his perfidy swept through her mind, felt torn in two, through her feelings towards him. She could have coped with this strange wedding, this business of the County being there after all; she could even have coped with Minerva's malicious tiny smile and the enigmatic expression on Howard's mother's face: two women who knew something that was affording them – if not amusement – then at least breathless interest in what Ann would do when she, too, discovered, what it was they knew.

No, she could cope with all that. What she couldn't cope with was the thought that Howard would leave her when he felt like it, to be with Felicity or someone like her, because he *wanted* to. The fact that neither Felicity, Tania nor Tom had been invited to the wedding, made no difference. Felicity had hinted that Howard had invited her out with him that evening and Ann had to believe it, because Howard was so impatient of Ann herself, and so eager to get away from Kingsbride to some unspecified place with some stranger that nobody was ever given a name for. Felicity, Tania perhaps, Minerva surely…

And after all, after his promises that there would be no honeymoon, Ann was swept away in the big dark limousine after the reception, shattered by the hollow mockery of showers of confetti and silver paper horseshoes, and the memory of young Opal's unhappy eyes and new defensive manner with Ann. What had been said to that child?

Ann expected they would catch a plane to some exotic place, that being Howard's style; instead, they went to a popular hotel on a sheltered part of the coast near Lamorna. Howard said, with distaste, in answer to her question, 'I now happen to own it, and as I promised you a honey-moonless marriage, it seemed a good idea to mix business with this enforced absence from Kingsbride.'

They had the best suite. Two separate luxurious bedrooms, two separate impossibly ornate bathrooms and a big connecting sitting-room. 'Well, don't say you don't like it,' he said, in what could only be termed a lightly mocking tone.

Ann didn't understand his manner. She

didn't know about the affectionate telegram Tom had unwisely sent, or what Minerva had said about it. 'Of course I don't like it,' Ann said. 'It's … it's vulgar. If we had to make a pretence of a honeymoon, why not a little place somewhere?'

'One feels as if one was in a goldfish bowl, in a small place.'

'And how come you own this sort of hotel, so suddenly?' Ann demanded.

He hunched his shoulders. 'Your mysterious illness, the worry over that child's escapades, so much work to be done – somehow I haven't had a chance to tell you. It just happens to be part of an inheritance that came to me.'

Things clicked into place in Ann's mind. She stood slim and straight and uncompromising, in her new going away outfit, chosen by Gertrude because of the way she appeared in that shrewd person's eyes; the suit made Ann into a stranger – a cool, self-confident and not very loving stranger, Howard thought. He wasn't surprised when that stranger remarked, in a voice dripping with chips of ice, 'Oh, yes, I believe I heard something about what you would get if you found a convenient wife to look after Opal for you and ask no questions. A business wife.'

Her words flicked him like the tip of a whip. 'Is there anything wrong in inheriting for services rendered?' he asked, deliberately couching his words to echo her own sentiments.

She had prayed that he would deny having such an inheritance. 'Yes. They're despicable,' she retorted.

'Even though, as I believe you were swift to point out, it was for Opal?'

Strange, Ann thought afterwards, how easily a quarrel could flare up between herself and his man, yet she had been so adept in the past at avoiding a quarrel, even with Felicity. Things went from bad to worse.

Shocked, she heard herself saying, in a bitter little voice that surely wasn't her own, 'Nothing's right about this marriage. I thought it was to be a quiet affair, in a Registry, with just two witnesses and no publicity. Somebody doesn't want it to happen and I got so ill I nearly died. Then you threw it open to the wide world, to see this impossible shaming marriage, with press included, and you broke your word about the honeymoon! Why, why?'

He hadn't broken his word about that, and he was hurt. 'Perhaps it was because I wanted to protect you from people's wagging tongues,' he said, equally angry. 'Had you thought of that?'

'I can't see how that could be your reason, or you would surely not have been so blatant in your attentions to my cousin Felicity.'

Now she was going too far. He came swiftly over to her. 'You'd better explain that, I think.'

She laughed, recklessly now. She was afraid of the intimate air of this suite that could surely have been designed for nothing else but a bridal pair, a rich bridal pair. She wanted to get out into the fresh air, and to find a stark little room where she could sleep alone without troubled thoughts and feelings about this very masculine and handsome man who was now her husband. A little too late, she realised that as it had been a proper marriage in the eyes of the world, it now gave him the usual rights of any husband, if he cared to break his word to her. And it looked as if he meant to.

She said, fighting hard, 'My cousin boasted about the way she caught your fancy, but she really didn't need to boast. I believed her. I've seen her in action before, and I don't suppose you're different from any other man.'

'Don't you? Don't you, indeed!' He caught her by the shoulders and held her roughly to him, and for a sick shrinking moment she thought that he was about to hurt her. One part of her wanted madly to be kissed by him, but the rest of her wouldn't forget Felicity's boasting and Minerva's smug smile.

Ann tried to break away from him,

resisting with every ounce of strength she had, but her resistance merely seemed to anger him.

He stared down at her, his fingers biting into her shoulders, and his anger sharpened to a degree that frightened him. 'That's what you do, isn't it?' he said, in a voice unlike his own. 'Drive men on with that young untouched look about you, goading them with the things you say – apparently reasonable things but with an unmistakable barb underneath – and then when they're wild, you hold them off. The frost maiden, cool, indifferent! Isn't that so?'

'I don't know what you're talking about!' Ann gasped, really scared now. 'You made me a promise. Why are you being like this?'

He controlled himself with an effort. 'I'm your husband, remember?'

So he really was going back on his word, she thought, with a sinking heart. 'In name only!' she snapped back, and as she saw the result of that, it gave her the boldness to add, '*You* remember! A business arrangement!' White, rigid with her anger, she continued, 'I only wanted a job, a roof over my head, and I consider I've been tricked into something I don't understand and which you most unfairly won't explain, even now. It's especially unfair, as everyone else seems to know about it. I can tell, from the way they look at me. But I'll hold you to your bargain. For Opal, you said, and it's just a business marriage. Not one whit more.'

He looked at the furious sparkle in her usually cool eyes, and then his own eyes dropped to her mouth: tender, untouched, appealing. Too appealing... He felt that if he looked at it any longer, he would drown in its sweetness, and not be responsible for his actions.

He thrust her away from him and marched to the door, went out, and just managed by a tremendous effort, to avoid slamming it behind him. But his going had such a tremendous finality about it, that Ann felt there was nothing left for her, anywhere. Nothing.

ELEVEN

The weather lost its cold sunshine; and rain, steady and unrelenting, set in. Howard took Ann about as if they were an undemonstrative but quite normal married couple. Ann was astonished that people looking at them in smiling approval couldn't realise that she was chill with anguish, at Howard's cold manner and his absence from her when there was no cause for them to appear in public. She didn't remember much of Lamorna except that its dripping trees, humid atmosphere and wet lush undergrowth seemed to echo to the skies her own stark unhappiness. But Howard was unrelenting at the programme prepared for them that week-end. He took meals with her, choosing carefully and consulting the wine waiter (but this was merely because he was a new hotel owner, she told herself) and he drove her around in the new limousine. He was a good driver and he showed her a lot of the county she had never seen. But when they were alone he was frigidly polite and left her as soon as he could.

They returned to Kingsbride on a day that was so cold, Ann was glad of the fire in her bedroom. At her own request she had been allowed to stay in the room next to Opal's, for the time being. She went in search of the child right away, but Opal was nowhere to be found. Instead, Howard's mother sent for her.

There was a difference in Mrs Crayne's manner. 'Now you are my daughter-in-law,' she began, 'I wish you to learn to become the chatelaine of Kingsbride. You must, in spite of what my son has said about this not being a normal marriage. And nobody, nobody outside these four walls must know, or learn why. You understand?'

Ann set her lips. 'I'm not willing to take part in a social existence, Mrs Crayne,' she said clearly. 'I am here for Opal's benefit, and I haven't yet been told the reason for the marriage. Not the whole truth, that is: the secret of Opal's birth.'

Mrs Crayne smiled faintly. 'You'll learn it, soon enough; perhaps without any help from me,' and there was a sinister ring in her tones.

'How shall I learn it since no one will tell me?'

'You'll learn it from the child herself.'

'But Opal doesn't know!'

'Perhaps not. I didn't say she would *tell* you. But you'll learn soon enough. We know who her parents were and why she must never be sent to school. She'll be all right so long as she is kept away from other children, and the danger of her being teased and frustrated. Keep her calm. That is your job. But for the family's sake it must remain hidden, and so you must behave as a normal wife of my son's.' Her thin-lipped smile ended the conversation. 'Socially.'

When Howard's mother finished a conversation, it was truly finished. Ann found herself meekly leaving the room. But outside the door, she ran into Gertrude.

'How can I find Opal? Where does she get to? You know, don't you?' Ann said furiously. 'I must get to the bottom of this, or else I can't go on!'

'I don't know,' Gertrude denied slowly, 'but Jago might tell you. Otherwise, I can only suggest you give all your time to being with Opal and following her.'

It was too ridiculous. Ann found Opal in her room. 'I was waiting for you,' she told Ann and she wore her surly look.

'How about,' Ann began, 'now I'm back–'

'From your honeymoon, with my Uncle Howard! You promised you wouldn't leave me!' Opal stormed.

'But I thought you wanted me to marry him! Anyway, I have to do most things he says,' Ann told her. 'But otherwise I thought you and I were good friends, and I have spent a lot of time searching for you. Where do you get to? And no outrageous stories, mind. The truth!'

'If you're not going to believe me, what's the use?' Opal muttered.

Ann sighed and saw she must abandon it for the time being. But Opal settled down to Ann's routine of lessons, walks on the moors with Jago and the animals. One or two had been taken away from him but the puppy and kitten were still for Ann.

Ann, who remembered uncomfortably how she had nearly lost her life on the moor, was glad of Jago with them, and occasionally they found a wounded animal to mend, and Jago showed them fascinating things such as hidden nests and shy little animals fleeing for cover, things a casual walker would miss. All seemed comfortable until one day when they returned, Mrs Farraker was waiting for them, with rather an odd look.

'Have you been out with my son, Jago, ma'am?' she asked unaccountably.

Ann was surprised. 'You know we take him, Opal and I, for safety. He knows the moor and we don't.'

Mrs Farraker seemed about to say something else but stopped, and without a word she pushed the child towards the stairs and led Ann to the library where she announced her to a room full of people. Ann, conscious of her untidy appearance, felt the housekeeper might have warned her, until she saw that the people were a very irritated Howard, his mother, Minerva, the vicar, the local doctor, and only two strangers – two elderly women in felt hats and worn tweeds and heavy shoes.

Howard said, without waiting for the others to begin, 'Ann, for heaven's sake, where have you been, and with whom?'

'I've been walking with Opal, as usual, with Jago and the animals.'

Minerva delicately shrugged and smiled at everyone. Ann said, 'If you'd rather I went out without Jago, and risked getting into difficulties, Howard, you only have to say. I've been in one dyke. I don't know the moor.'

'Heavens, Ann, do you have to take such wild walks? What's wrong with taking the child for a drive – you and Opal in the back getting maximum fresh air and Burridge driving and seeing that you come to no harm.'

'I'll tell you,' she said coldly, 'if we may have a private conversation. I don't quite see why...' and she looked pointedly round, skimming lightly over the faces of his mother and Minerva, which were inevitable, and resting lightly on the face of the doctor, finally scowling at the vicar and the two women.

It appeared that they were relatives of the vicar's; two women who loved village gossip and had gleaned a lot about the way Jago lost his temper and looked rather dangerous in certain circumstances. They added that it didn't seem quite nice for Howard's wife to be seen around in the company of a simpleton.

Ann rarely lost her temper but there were so many aspects of this scene that displeased her. The number of people suddenly and without warning facing her on this issue; the fact that Howard's mother had an interest in it and was looking more angry than usual, and Minerva's faint trace of malice in her smile when her head was carefully turned from Howard, were no less irritating to Ann than the fact that two strange females had been listened to before Ann's own husband had spoken to her about it.

She realised that Minerva wanted to see her lose her temper so she stood there, woodenly, until they had all finished saying things.

'Well?' Howard barked, but Ann merely continued to stare silently at him.

She wondered, afterwards, if she could have been said to have won that round. People can be made to look rather silly when the victim won't answer. But Howard's anger when he finally did talk to her alone, was a new thing. He just wouldn't let her speak, and when she insisted, he raised his voice, drowning hers. So she did the only thing she felt she could, and marched to the door, only to find him standing with his back to it, barring her way.

'Just what do you want of me?' she asked, when he was finally silent. 'I am doing my best in a very difficult situation. But that sort of scene in there was unpardonable. Unfair. Disgraceful! What's *wrong* with Jago as a bodyguard for me?'

'Never mind about that!' he snapped, losing all sense of proportion. He had had a bad time with his mother, and Minerva's interest was puzzling even the easy-going Howard. Ann's safety was paramount with him, and when strangers had been brought in as anxious onlookers, he felt it had all gone too far. 'If I say you are not to go out with Jago in your party, then you do as I say!'

'I refuse!' she said. Her voice was low and clear, and a look in her eyes that he hadn't seen before. 'I am prepared to believe that at first this marriage seemed a good idea to you, but you've weakly let others interfere and now it's all gone too far. So far as I'm concerned, it's finished.'

'What do you mean?' he asked, whitening. 'It can't finish. You're my wife.'

'Perhaps you don't know that the people in the kitchen (so I hear in a round-about way) have heard your dear friend Minerva giving her opinion that as the marriage hasn't been consummated, you can rid yourself of me at any time you like. I don't know how she knows. But that apart, I imagine that what applies to you, applies to me. It was no marriage and it never will be, so I say it finishes.'

He took hold of her arm. 'Who told you Minerva said such a thing? I don't believe she would, not even Minerva!'

'Don't you! She tried to stop the wedding, by persuading my cousin to give me something to make me ill. You don't believe that, do you? But I know Felicity – I know how rotten she can be to me, but I know she wouldn't go as far as that!'

'And I am equally sure Minerva wouldn't!' Howard stormed. 'You said yourself it was something you ate, and now you're making up wild stories because you don't like Minerva. And how come the kitchen staff got into it?'

Ann let her attention wander, to the point that it was an odd thing, the 'voices in the air' Opal so staunchly held to. She looked up at the ancient walls of this, one of the rooms in the old part of Kingsbride. Was it possible that there were holes in all that complicated carved pattern in the panelling, through which things said could filter? Was it possible that the sounds could be directed down to the kitchen regions?

'Ann! Listen to me! It isn't true, is it?'

'I don't care whether it's true or not. I'm

finished here. Let's just agree to part. You've got what you wanted, a huge inheritance for taking Opal. Don't keep tearing me to pieces any longer.'

He let her go then, with the memory of her still white face and wide eyes, as she had been looking up at the panelling, vivid in his mind. He hadn't approached it in the right way. Of course she was furious! There must be a better way to talk this thing over, if only his jealousy at Minerva's implications about Ann could be tamped down. But Minerva had suggested that Ann had been using Jago as 'escort' to look after Opal while Ann slipped away with Tom Westbury. He couldn't push that out of his mind. He had seen the way Ann had looked at Westbury that last time; how her face had lit. He couldn't accept that it was just delight at seeing the face of an old friend, because Ann was lost and unhappy in this place. Kingsbride was Howard's home. He loved it and couldn't see why Ann shouldn't also love it. He knew his mother had spoken to her about being groomed to be chatelaine here.

He went in search of Ann, to try again, and when he couldn't find her, he went to speak to Minerva, but she had taken refuge in his mother's room, and they were talking and refused to be disturbed. Gertrude told him so.

He looked at Gertrude with new eyes. Was she friend or foe? He recalled something Ann had said, on that ill-fated 'honeymoon', that Gertrude was warm-hearted underneath that forbidding exterior. It had seemed so incongruous at the time. Now he clung to the desperate straw of the truth in Ann's words. 'Do you like Ann?' he asked bluntly.

Gertrude closed the door behind her, and nodded.

'Will you help her? She's in deep trouble.'

'I know,' Gertrude agreed, in a breath so soft that nobody could have heard but himself. 'But only you can help her, Mr Howard.'

'How?' he demanded.

Gertrude looked as if she would risk all in telling him, but his mother called to her and Minerva added her voice. Gertrude almost shrugged, and went in.

He decided to tackle Ann again, but her room was empty and so was the child's room. There was a cold lost sensation in both of these rooms, and he remembered how those two had looked, before the wedding day, the day Ann had been ill in bed and the child had gone to sleep cuddled in her arms. They would be together, he decided, but where?

Following Opal had paid off, Ann discovered, yet it was three days before the child led her to her hide-out. The light was fast draining out of the day and Kingsbride could be filled with threatening shadows in its many corridors. She had followed the child and concentrated on keeping well back in case Opal should instinctively feel she was being kept under surveillance, and look behind, and so Ann had not noticed where she was going. They had gone through doors with hinges so well-oiled that not the softest purr of a sound had emitted, and now Ann didn't know where she was. Somewhere where the windows were high, small and dirty, and there was the smell of age. All Ann could think of was that this was the disused wing, locked, left to spiders and layers of dust. Down on the same floor as that of Howard's mother's suite, yet it seemed they had traversed a mile to get there.

At last Opal had gone through a final door into a little room that had nothing but junk in it; the worn furniture of another age, too shabby to be of further use, not good enough to merit the expense of the services of the firm which sent people to examine the priceless pieces regularly and keep them in good condition. Opal went unerringly to a little light and turned it on, and as she realised she was not alone, she spun round and gasped. 'Oh, it's you!' she said, her surly look replacing the half-scared, half defensive one that the light had surprised.

'Opal, you're not friends with me again. What has someone said?' Ann asked.

Opal stood wooden, mulish, resisting Ann's loving arms. 'What's got into people?' Ann choked. 'I've had such a nasty time with a lot of people shouting at me for taking Jago out with us as bodyguard. Did you know about that?' and Opal nodded.

'Your "voices in the air!", I suppose,' Ann said with resignation.

Opal nodded fiercely. 'Yes, it is, and if you like, I'll show you where they come from and then perhaps you'll believe me, only I got disturbed and I didn't mark the way in and perhaps I won't be able to find it again. Don't look at me like that – it's true! I found out about it in an old book. I wasn't prying. I thought it was a geography book, but it was all about Kingsbride, with plans and things. That's how I found this place, and it's my own, my very own. At least it was, only someone's been here. I didn't mean you! I know it wasn't you! You wouldn't turn over my things. But someone has,' and Opal started to cry, that piteous uncontrolled crying that had once before torn at Ann's heart.

'My dear, don't,' she begged presently, when her comforting did nothing to stop the harsh dry sobs. 'You'll make yourself sick and ill. What do *things* matter?'

'Well, they do! At least, these things do,' Opal choked.

'Tell me about them,' Ann persuaded the child, as she looked round at the dusty cobwebby place in distaste. This was no place for a child to play in.

'My things, that belonged to my mother,' 'Opal said at last.

Ann sat back on her heels. 'Now look here, you said you didn't know who you were or anything about your past life.'

'I know,' Opal shrugged. 'You won't believe me. Why should you? Only, well, I *found* these things, and they had my name on, so they were mine, weren't they?'

'What things and where did you find them?' Ann asked sternly.

Opal looked doubtfully at her. 'This is true,' she said in a scared whisper. 'No made up stories. All true. See, when that last woman didn't want me any more a man came and took me to the big house. They said it was to see my great-uncle. Only he was dead and I couldn't see him. You've got to believe me, Ann! It was at his house and there were a lot of people in black and there was this big room full of books. They put me in there to wait, with my suitcase, and someone brought me some milk and biscuits, only they said don't move and I was all alone and it was such a long time and so boring. I got fed up with waiting and not moving so I got up and looked at some things.'

She reddened under Ann's straight looks. 'Well, all right, I was nosey and I poked about at the big desk and a drawer flew open and hit me in the chest and hurt me, only there was this box inside and it said "Opal Guinevere" and something about "To be opened on my death" and – well, it said *to me*. I was Opal Guinevere so I opened it.'

Ann said nothing. It had the sound and smell of Opal's wild exaggerated stories. The child must have thought so, for she turned round and scrabbled under a lot of cardboard boxes, and brought out a box. 'This is it, only someone's been at it. I know because the things have been turned over and the black cotton thread broken. You can always tell. And the letter's been opened. Look!' Outrage was in her voice and she started crying again. 'I don't care about the glass beads and things being touched. It was the letter. It said to be opened when I was 17 and I was going to wait till then, honest. Especially as I can't read people's rotten writing anyway,' she added, honestly.

Ann stared at the letter. 'Here, you read it,' Opal said, thrusting it at her.

It was on expensive paper, with the address embossed in a slightly darker shade of the greyish-brown of the paper: a familiar address. Ann remembered suddenly that this address would be the manor house where the old great-uncle had lived, the one who had been so angry about this child, Ann recalled.

'Read it aloud,' Opal prompted, with good reason. The writing was almost illegible. Ann battled with it, and read, slowly, haltingly, 'My very dear daughter,' and Opal sighed a great sigh and leaned hard against Ann.

'I am ill. I have so little time left, and I don't want anyone else to tell you this story but myself,' the writer went on. 'I have been so ill and I am not going to recover, and there is a great deal of money which will come to you, pet, and I want you to have it.'

Opal paused in her attempts to clean her new spectacles and murmured ecstatically, 'My mother – she says so!'

Ann nodded and continued, 'Nothing must stand in the way of that, and so I am going to hide this letter under the things in this box I leave for you. It will be sealed. I don't want Uncle or the legal men or my husband to know about it. It is a secret for you only.'

Secrets. The breath of life to Opal, just like her mother, Ann thought, as she pulled the child closer to her side.

But the letter was not, it appeared to be a happy one, and Ann thought she would never be able to erase the sight of the look of wonder draining away from Opal's young face, as she heard that the dying woman who had penned that letter was not her mother at all.

'My own daughter died, but we didn't let Uncle know, because of the inheritance. Somehow we found you, a child belonging to nobody, and looking reasonably like our own. Too young to betray the truth of who you were, yet with the right colouring and features near enough to our Opal's to fool Uncle. Only my husband had a secret, too, and now I must tell you (and you must believe me!) that you are not his daughter, because there is in his family...'

Having struggled so far, it was terrible to them to find that the page which should have continued the saga, wasn't there. Opal shrieked, 'Where's the rest?' and then she bitterly said, 'Someone took it!' She had evidently thought someone had merely opened the letter, read it and put it back. They searched through the box together. The secret bottom was cleverly made, and only Opal's prying fingers could have found it. 'Did you put the letter back in that secret place last time you looked at it?' Ann asked the child.

'No. I'd only been looking at it – not opening it–' Opal confessed. 'I couldn't wait.'

It was an awful confession. Ann wondered why that woman, who had called herself this child's mother, had set the date for opening such a letter, so far ahead. Opal offered, 'Well, it was mine, mine! And people keep saying there's a secret about my birth and Uncle Howard hates me and so does everyone except you and now he'll make you hate me because you're his wife...'

'My dear, nobody can make a person hate someone else,' Ann said quietly, but with such conviction that Opal turned round to search her face. It was heartbreaking, the way the child tried to read the truth of that. 'Now you must know that's so, Opal, love. You must know very well that I wouldn't have gone out to find you that night ... where were you, by the way? Here? Is this where you hid?'

Opal nodded. 'And you nearly died and they said it was my fault,' she sobbed.

'Well, it's all in the past now, but this isn't. This is very important. Can you show me the other things that were left for you?' and she turned to what had appeared to be a necklace of white stones, carelessly flung in the box. Opal said indifferently, 'These glass beads and things.'

Ann lifted the necklace and her heart missed a beat. She didn't know a precious stone from a fake, but there was no mistaking the quality and beauty of the design of that necklace nor the excellence of the setting of each stone. A diamond necklace

worth a fortune, Ann found herself thinking. There was a bracelet, ear-rings and
rings to match. Opal said casually that she
played with them sometimes. It didn't
matter, they were for her, weren't they?'

'Yes, but...' Ann began, thinking of the
solicitors to the estate. But the woman who
had written that letter had said definitely
she didn't want the legal men to know,
hadn't she? And surely the person who owns
the things has the right to say who shall
know and who shall not? 'But where is the
ending of the letter? Who was it from? Can
you remember, Opal? Could you read her
signature?'

Opal didn't know how Ann guessed she
had unsealed the letter, to try and read it. It
wasn't worth bothering about. She shook
her head. 'I couldn't read any of it. Why
didn't she do it in capital letters?'

'She was very, very ill,' Ann said on a low
note. 'And whereabouts in here did you
keep your box of treasures?'

'Under this loose floorboard,' Opal said,
displaying it.

'How did you bring a box this size from
the old Uncle's house?'

Opal explained. 'I put it in a bag in my
suitcase, before they came for me.' The old
cloth bag with the draw-string, which had
been the repository for her few bits and
pieces, in each of the places that she

remembered living in. Her quick wits had told her nobody would search in there, where she kept her 'rubbish'.

'But I didn't put it back under the floor-boards last time. I thought I heard some-body at the door, so I went to look and I sort of forgot to hide the box. I just came out and got washed for lunch so nobody would ask where I'd been.'

Minerva, Ann thought instinctively. It was just the sort of thing that woman would do. She had all the time in the world and she was bent on getting rid of both Ann and this child.

'What are we going to do?' Opal whisp-ered. 'Who's got the end of my letter?'

Ann sighed. 'There's only one thing to do, my dear, if you want to find it again. I must tell your Uncle Howard about this.' She hushed the child's instant cry of protest. 'What else can we do?' Ann asked, so reason-ably that even Opal's voice was stilled.

TWELVE

It was some hours before Ann could find Howard alone and then it was in the stables. He and Minerva had just ridden in, and as always, Minerva was in a great hurry to return to the house and get out of her riding clothes. Howard had stayed behind to groom his horse and keep an eye on the lad doing Minerva's.

Ann said tautly, 'I have something very important to say to you.'

'What, here?' Howard asked sharply. His eyes raked her hungrily. She was slim as a boy, neat in a starkly plain dark dress, and her hair – combed back and pristine neat – shone in the waning light. He noticed she wore little make-up, and she looked fresh, good enough to eat.

As always, it made him angry. The longer this marriage went on, the more difficult it would be to change it to the one of warmth and friendship that he daily craved more and more. And he was powerless to make the first move. He knew it. He was as he was; formal, undemonstrative. What moves he had been able to make had already been made, and had been of no avail. And daily

Minerva kept hinting, dropping little hints that didn't seem to mean much at the time but later made him wonder; was Minerva totally wrong, or was there some reason why Westbury was still hanging around, when he should be off to take up that job of his? And now today Minerva had said casually that Westbury had given up that job and was waiting to see what Ann was intending to do.

He called to the boy. 'Finish this for me,' he said, and to Ann, 'Let's walk. Let's find somewhere private, if we can. I've things to say to you, too.'

Minerva watched them go to the path through the copse to the clifftops, from his mother's window.

'Why didn't you do something to prevent it?' Mrs Crayne demanded. 'You said you could handle this, but look at it! My son still looks at her as if nothing in the world will persuade him to have that marriage annulled. For all I know, it may already be too late!'

'No, it isn't that,' Minerva said with satisfaction. 'Of that, I can assure you. The maid at the hotel reported that they slept miles apart, and the whole staff was talking about it. Two miserable people who certainly didn't have a honeymoon. And Zoë keeps an eye on things here.'

'Well, they've gone off together now!' his

mother snapped.

'Yes, but the way they departed, it's hardly likely that anything will change. They both looked quite hostile, as usual.'

Hostile. The word leapt into Howard's mind as he looked down into Ann's face. They had pulled up at the Kingsbride boundary, and stood leaning against one of the many dry walls that are a feature of the county. The wind buffeted them and nothing was comfortable anywhere, and Ann looked at him as if she hated him.

'Well, what was it *you* wanted to say?' he asked her, wondering how he could put into words his question about herself and Tom Westbury.

Ann got out from her pocket the letter, but put it back again. How to begin? Howard made up her mind for her by quickly helping himself to it. She watched his face turn ashen as he recognised the handwriting. 'How did you get hold of this?'

'As you've decided to take the letter for yourself, Howard, the careful explanation I was trying to frame is now irrelevant, so I recommend you to read it for yourself,' she said coolly. He did, quickly and with ease, no doubt from past familiarity with the writing, she thought. Then, 'Where's the rest?' he demanded.

'That is what I want *you* to find out,' she retorted. 'As you see, it was intended for

244

Opal – *our* Opal – and someone has been to her box of treasures, read that letter, and taken part of it.'

'Read it! Oh, really, Ann!'

'As you see from the envelope, it mentions the age of seventeen and she intended to keep it for then, but she was so unhappy, she went to it today, deciding to read it after all. She's as unhappy as I am about all these innuendos about the secret of her birth. Who can blame her? But the thing is, somebody knew where she kept her box of treasures. Somebody found out how the bottom of the box opened, and got this out. Somebody knows now, what we don't know ... what was the meaning of the last...'

'Just a minute,' Howard broke in. '*Where* was this kept? What was the box of treasures you're talking about? And how came Opal to have possession of this letter anyway?'

Ann sighed. 'You won't let me explain things in my own way, will you? I was going to, only you took the letter and insisted on reading it.' He looked stormy for a moment, then he shrugged and let her take her time. She told him how she had followed Opal, discovered where she had hidden the day that Ann had fallen into the dyke, and got the rest of the story from her today. 'No, stay here. Let us be alone for once, without fear of Minerva interrupting,' Ann said sharply as he turned to go back to Kingsbride, no doubt with the intention of seeking Opal out to have an angry scene with her. 'Don't you see, Howard? She not unnaturally wants to know who she is. You can't ... you just can't get angry with her now. Why? Because she's just discovered that you're not her uncle. She isn't related to this family at all. She's what she expected to be found to be, from the first: an unwanted orphan, from nobody knows where. Unwanted, unloved ... except by me,' she added, in a low intense voice.

Howard stared at her, trying to think clearly. 'All right, you seem to be so sure that the rest of this letter was stolen. Who by?'

'You want me to say Minerva, don't you? But ask yourself – who else would have any interest in it?'

'My mother,' he said, in a hard voice, and Ann was shocked to see what it had cost him to say that. 'My mother would send someone to search the child's things.'

'No,' Ann contradicted, thinking hard. 'She couldn't. She can only claim allegiance from Gertrude, and Gertrude wouldn't do this. Gertrude likes Opal and is my friend. No, it would be Minerva. It must have been!'

'Don't be absurd. Why should she do such a thing?'

'Don't ask me why she does it, but she does. At least, she has me followed. She has talked to Tom Westbury about me. She likes intrigues.'

'Westbury!' It was most unfortunate that his name was mentioned. Howard's face flamed. 'Yes, that was what I wanted to talk to you about,' he said.

'Well, don't bother!' she flashed. 'I'll tell you what you want to know. Tom is apparently still hanging around here in case I need him because he's worried about me. And do you know why? Because of all the hints and doubts that Minerva keeps dropping into his ears. She's made him think you're horrible to me and that I'd do anything to get away, and poor old Tom is waiting, to be there, when you have this marriage annulled.'

'Yes, you mentioned it before – the kitchen staff heard about it, I think you said. But how did *you* find out what the kitchen staff think they heard?'

She whitened. 'Opal told me. She was upset and sure I'm going to be sent away which is her way of putting it. Well, you must have said it to someone! *Someone* must have said it. Say what you like about people listening at keyholes, but if things weren't *said,* eavesdropping wouldn't be worthwhile!'

'We shall have to find out how people do hear so much of what is said in private, won't we?' he said bitterly. 'Yes, it has been mooted, but not by me. I don't know how people hear these things, since I've just remembered there are no keyholes in those doors below your floor, but yes, I did mention it. I said, in fact, that never in a hundred years would I have this marriage annulled. So yes, I did mention that word but in the negative sense. I suppose something could be made of it!'

They were walking again. It was getting cold. Ann hugged her arms to her chest because of the rising wind, that accompanied the wild incoming tide. The coastline looked unfriendly, and above the cliffs what could be seen of Kingsbride looked frankly sinister. Glancing back at it, Ann thought of things like prisons, fortresses, dungeons, but never a home. 'I love Opal and I would like to take her away from Kingsbride. So if you want the marriage annulled, go ahead with it, but let me keep that poor child!'

Howard stopped, amazed. 'Go ahead with breaking up a marriage I've worked so hard to bring about? You must be mad. Certainly not. And I'm not going to give you your freedom to go off with Westbury, either.'

'He'd make a better husband than you are!' Ann said, and realised that that was a thought she hadn't even admitted to herself. Tom would make a woman with an unwanted child, a good husband. Only, she thought, tears crowding her eyes, stinging with the salt in the wind already – the sad thing was that she didn't want good, kind

Tom, who would be so respectable, responsible, kind, everything a child like Opal would want in a father. No, Ann thought bleakly, as they walked faster against the wind, she was hooked; madly, wretchedly in love with this man, who had no warmth in him, only arrogance, and his beastly sense of what was fitting.

'What are you going to do about finding the rest of that letter?'

'Nothing,' he said at once. 'You want to know the significance of that last sentence, don't you, and I know the answer to that already. But it won't do you any good, or Opal. In fact, now we can send her away to school, which is what Minerva is always sensibly advising.'

'Is she indeed! Well, you can cut out the word "sensibly". Minerva wants to get rid of Opal because she can see that the child and I–'

'Exactly. The child needs companions of her own age.'

'Why now, if not before? Goodness,' she said, thinking, 'you need never have put that advertisement in the newspaper. No, wait a minute – I've heard it somewhere that you stood to inherit a lot of money by taking Opal. That was all you wanted, wasn't it?'

He stopped and took her shoulders in a hard grip. 'What if I did inherit a lot of money? What's wrong with money? Why do you despise money so much?'

'I don't know, but I do. That horrible hotel that we went to for our so-called honeymoon – that came by courtesy of your adopting Opal, didn't it?'

He let his hands drop at the word 'honeymoon' and he said heavily, 'Actually, no. You're getting muddled. It was another relative's legacy altogether. And if you will look at Kingsbride closely, thoughtfully, you will see that it is like a monster, devouring every penny that comes into my pockets.'

'Then why continue to live there?' she wondered. 'Why not sell it?'

'How *could* you? It's my home. For centuries my family has lived there. I will go on keeping it, starve to keep it, if I must.' He looked thoughtfully at her. 'I suppose you want a little house in a row of neat little houses, with Westbury. Is that it?'

'Tom again! Why, you're jealous of poor Tom – that's it, isn't it? He has more to offer any woman than you with your money and your mansion!' Despair drove her now. She didn't care what she said. 'And you don't play fair. You haven't told me what that last sentence means in the letter.'

She was sorry the minute she had said it. His face mirrored not just anger but all the unhappiness and horror any human being can call up on the instant.

'All right, I'll tell you. No doubt you've

heard about my tragic love affair. That will be another "voice in the air", according to Opal. Somehow you think the person in that old love affair was Minerva. I can assure you, I have never wanted to marry her. She was engaged to me on the rebound, from someone else I wanted to get over. Minerva knew that, and in the end she left me for her rich man she taunted me that she could find. And now she's a widow she thinks she can take up where she left off, because the other one is dead. The one who wrote this letter. Elaine...'

He said the name as if he were forcing himself to say it, but once it had rolled off his tongue, he seemed relieved, surprised to find it so. It had haunted him for years. *Elaine...*'he said again, and Ann shivered as the wind tore the name away from his lips. 'I don't seem to be very good with women,' he said, wryly. 'Elaine left me for my best friend, Colin. They married and had a child, and it wasn't until then that we learned that there was a shaky history of mental illness in his family. Tainted. And Elaine was allowed to find out somehow. Beautiful, unhappy Elaine...'

Ann had to run to keep up with him. Now intermittent spots of rain began to fall, but he didn't seem to notice. It was as if demons were urging him on. Ann moved at his pace, over the bluff, and almost down to the next village, before he realised how the sky had darkened, and the weather was worsening. He had a jacket on, from his riding; Ann had no coat at all. She was chilled through and through but she was determined to say nothing about it.

'So Elaine suffered,' he continued as he strode along. 'I don't know what happened. The lawyer wanted to tell me but I wouldn't listen. Elaine and Colin died in a car accident.'

'But I thought she died of an illness,' Ann said involuntarily.

'Ill she may have been, but she was in the car with her husband the day she died. They were quarrelling, witnesses said, and he took his eyes off the road. Nobody knows what they were quarrelling about, but the child couldn't be found afterwards. The old man traced her at last, and left her with her foster-mother, till he died. In the light of this letter, it looks as if their baby died in infancy and they hastily adopted another one. Why, why?' he asked of himself.

It was stated clearly in the part of the letter they had that it was because of the inheritance. Ann supposed he couldn't bring himself to believe that. She couldn't hurt Howard by pointing it out to him, but let him think otherwise. 'I suppose Elaine missed her baby so much and needed another one,' he said. 'I've heard of such cases before.' He pushed his wet hair back from his forehead, and discovered it was raining. Impatiently he flicked droplets off his shoulders and they strode down into the village. 'The thing is, Opal isn't that child! She hasn't inherited that taint from Colin's family. So we don't now have to worry about *that,* which was the reason why we dare not send her away to school. Heaven knows what *will* come out in her,' he finished gloomily, 'since we don't know who she was or where they found her. But she *isn't Elaine's child.*'

'And so you won't care now, what happens to her,' Ann said fiercely.

At her voice, he turned and looked at her, as if he had forgotten she was there beside him. Just aware there had been someone to listen to his anguished outpourings. 'Good heavens, you've no coat! Why didn't you say so?'

'Would you have cared?' Ann retorted.

She shrank from his anger. She thought he was going to take her by the shoulders and shake her. But there was an interruption. A farmer drove by, came to a halt, and called to them. 'Lor bless us, Mr Crayne, get caught on a walk, did you? Your lady's fair wet through. Hop in. We're near my place. The missus'll get you dry things.'

'No, thanks, we'd rather go home,' Howard protested, but the man wouldn't

253

hear of it. He said he was almost on his own doorstep.

Ann couldn't stop shivering, and now Howard was all contrite. 'Heavens, why did this have to happen?' he muttered. 'So soon on the other business. Are you feeling all right?' and he put a hand on her hot head. She flinched away, her eyes blazing. She didn't want him to touch her or come near her.

The farmer noticed nothing. They were newly-weds, he was well aware, and he liked them both. He was happy to take them to his home.

From out of the cold grey wet noisy evening, the farmhouse kitchen was a haven of warmth, bustle and good cooking smells. Ann was received with delight and swept off upstairs to a bedroom that had a big gas-fire. The warmth seeped into her bones and she was given the quickest hot bath of her life and enveloped into a huge fluffy bath towel, the farmer's wife garrulously talking about the early days of her married life when she didn't understand the moor and often got caught out in inclement weather. 'You'll learn, m'dear,' she chuckled. 'And you'll learn about your man, too. Always looks angry, Mr Howard, and always has done, but he's one of the best. Right glad we were to see the bride he'd chose. Thought it was going to be that painted doll who was engaged to him before.'

Ann wanted so badly to know all about it, but it was not in her nature to question a neighbour. 'Minerva's staying with us now,' she said distantly, hoping it would stop gossip, but the farmer's wife said, 'I didn't mean that hussy. I meant the other one. Elaine. Ah, she was the one to turn men's heads. Been brought up together, those two, and it was to be the wedding of the year. Only she ditched him for that friend of his. Friend!'

There was a huge king-size bed in the room. A girl came up with an old-fashioned warming pan and energetically forced it up and down between the sheets.

Ann said, 'Oh, but we must go back to Kingsbride. We can't stay here.'

The farmer's wife looked thoughtfully at the weather which had worsened in such a short while. 'Your man won't mind staying, I'll be bound. Came on foot, didn't you both? Well, there's lovers for you! He knows he shouldn't have kept on walking for so long, the sky changing like that! But he'll stay here, for sure. You'll see!'

'Oh, but please,' Ann urged. 'There's the child – she won't know where I am.'

'Well, there's the telephone,' the farmer's wife said reasonably. She hesitated. 'Don't mind if I give you a bit of advice, my dear. You're well-liked in the district, and in such a short while that's not usual for a stranger. It's from this liking that I'm sticking my neck out to give you advice. Remember always how bad your man's been treated, by everyone. There's men like that, who shoulder all the burdens, take the kicks, and not say nothing. But it goes deep. If he don't smile much, maybe that's because he's forgot how to smile. Give him warmth, m'dear. Thaw that load of ice he's put round himself to keep the world out. Show him that there's one woman he can love and trust. That's all I've got to say. And now I'll go down and dish up a nice warm supper for you both, up here, nice and quiet.' There didn't seem much more Ann could say, so she decided to leave it to Howard.

Howard came up a little later and diffidently knocked on the door. They had found him some clothes, thick husky home-knits and riding breeches. Farmers' gear, and it suited him. He looked bigger than ever. He towered over Ann, who was cuddled into a fluffy bathrobe and nothing much else. Her toes wiggled pink and warm on the fur rug before the fire, and her hair, combed out and almost dry, lay in a shining curtain over her shoulders. He had never seen her like this before.

He forgot what he had come to say. He took her face in his two hands and held it, so gently, and it seemed to Ann that he was, by his touch, drugging her, robbing her of her will, so that all she wanted was to stay here in the warmth and safety of one of the farmhouse bedrooms, so different from that hotel suite where they had spent such a strange week-end following their marriage.

Howard said very softly, 'You've put a spell on me. I wanted to stay angry, about Opal and Elaine and all the dead past, only you've driven it out. I can't even remember what Elaine looked like. I just worry about you, losing you to that chap Westbury. Have I really need to worry, Ann?'

It wasn't of her own volition that she shook her head. She wanted to say that she was sure of Tom and would rather go away with him, but the words wouldn't come. Howard said, 'You *are* my wife, and nothing anyone can say can alter that, and no matter how much you fight, I'm going to kiss you. I should have done it before,' and he gently laid his mouth on hers.

It was intended to be just a gentle kiss, a starting kiss, to see how she would take it, and to reassure himself that she wouldn't recoil from him with that new hating look in her eyes. What he hadn't bargain for was the way she went limp against him, her body seeming to have no more will to fight.

His arms tightened round her, taking her weight, and it seemed as if a flame had ignited between them. Afterwards she could only recall the urgent pressure of his mouth on hers, all over her face, urgent, questing, down her throat to the warm hollow at its base, until she felt she couldn't think any more. Distantly she heard footsteps outside the door, but Howard made no sign that he had heard. There was a soft knock on the door, and then the farmer's wife murmured to someone, with a fat chuckle, 'Reckon this stuff'll keep warm if we leave it here on the table like, with the covers on. They'll be hungry presently,' and then both sets of footsteps moved away. Ann felt herself lifted and carried towards the bed. Warmth was replaced by a wild excitement, and all coherent thought left her. This was the man she loved, the man she had married...

After the manner of the moor, the weather cleared suddenly. A shaft of too brilliant sunshine came through a gap in the heavy curtains and woke Ann, to find Howard was sitting on the side of the bed, fully dressed, watching her.

The memory of the night before came flooding back, and she slithered down under the sheets in a curiously endearing gesture, only her eyes, wide and questioning, remaining above. Howard laughed softly.

'You baby!' he said, and leaned down to kiss her. He ruffled her hair gently, with a hand that was, she noticed for the first time, strong yet slender, a beautifully kept hand, yet in some way a very masculine one.

She forced herself to say 'Good morning,' and the formality of the two words wiped the smile from his face. He removed his hand. 'You're sorry last night ever happened, aren't you,' he said, but it was a statement, not a question. All his built-in hurt rushed to the fore, and he got up and went to look out of the window. 'I've telephoned Kingsbride. Burridge will be bringing the car to pick us up, after breakfast. Will you have breakfast up here?'

Ann's heart sank. Why couldn't he have settled to walk back over the moor, and not have the car sent to meet them? Everybody would be looking out for them.

'I don't want to go back to Kingsbride this morning,' she said clearly.

He frowned. 'Why ever not? I thought you were so keen to be with Opal!'

That was another thing about Howard: endearing he might be, on occasion, but he didn't expect his wife to go against his plans and wishes. She said firmly: 'I have some shopping to do in town. It's a nice morning. I could go on the bus.'

'Well, they've dried your clothes, but as I remember it, you had no coat or gloves and certainly no handbag. What will you do for money?'

She sat up, holding the bedclothes close to

her. 'Perhaps you could give me some loose change, just to get into town. I have accounts there, if you remember.'

'I see,' Howard said, and obviously didn't see. In his mind, he had planned to take Ann home and straight to his mother; to tell her that this was no business marriage but the real thing, and moreover, to tell his mother to indicate to Minerva that her stay at Kingsbride was at an end. He couldn't do it himself because Minerva had said clearly that she was his mother's guest.

But on the whole, he thought, standing there watching the now quiet sea, almost at low tide, on the whole it might be better to have a showdown with his mother in Ann's absence. 'All right,' he decided. 'When Burridge comes, he'll drive you into town. I can walk back to Kingsbride. Yes, that's a better arrangement.'

In an odd sort of way, Ann was disappointed. She had the hazy desire for Howard to keep on insisting that she tell him what was wrong, and that in intimate fashion – not like this with half a room between them – she could confide in him, plan with him how they were to let Opal know that everything was now all right. They must make that poor child see that although she wasn't related to them, Ann wanted her officially adopted. If that were necessary? After all, the child had been officially adopted, she supposed, by Elaine and Colin.

Something of the same train of thought had been going through Howard's mind. 'I shall have to see the solicitor, of course, about Opal. For all I know, there are papers relating to what was to happen to her in any unforeseen eventuality. I must go to London,' he frowned.

She wanted to ask him if she could go with him, but she left it too long, and he said, half to himself, 'Minerva can travel with me. Yes, a very tidy way out,' but he forgot he hadn't told Ann that he was terminating Minerva's stay at Kingsbride that day. Ann naturally thought he meant he wanted Minerva's company on a pre-planned trip to Town.

Howard left Ann to get dressed, the warmth and intimacy of the night before now fled. She was very hungry, and recalled she had had no food last night. She went downstairs and found Howard just finishing breakfast. 'Have some of these kidneys and bacon,' he invited casually, and to the farmer's wife, 'They're good! We don't get food like that at Kingsbride.'

He got up to start out for his walk back. Ann, aware that the farmer's wife was doing her best to hide a lively interest in them both, panicked, and didn't want to be left alone with her. 'Won't you sit with me while I eat, Howard?'

He either didn't want to stay and act the buffer, or else his thoughts were elsewhere. He told her he hadn't the time. Ann heard him gracefully settling financially with the farmer's wife for the hospitality they had received. He did it with a kind of bulldozer manner mixed with pleasantness, that didn't permit of the woman refusing. The farmer's wife didn't try to. Besides, she had other things on her mind. What had happened last night, to make that poor child look so wretched?

But to Ann's infinite relief, Burridge came almost at once with the car, so she was able to go with him right away, saying she wasn't really hungry. Without actually running out to the car, she made enough speed to avoid questions.

Burridge looked at her thoughtfully, and away, quietly taking her instructions. He knew, she thought angrily. All the staff knew and would be speculating. Why had she not interrupted Howard's angry conversation while they were walking last night in order to turn back to Kingsbride before they got too wet and too far to do so? But if she had, she would not have heard that impassioned story of his old love, Ann was sure. Perhaps he was even regretting having told her, at this very moment. She looked out of the back window, but the Cornish terrain didn't allow backward glances. Howard, striding out towards Kingsbride, was already lost to view behind an outcrop of rocks. The moor had enfolded him, and the sea's whispering would muffle his footsteps. Gone, she whispered to herself, metaphorically as well as literally. It seemed impossible that she would be able to snatch back the magic of last night. And she forgot that Minerva had now lost her trump card; she couldn't hope to see the marriage annulled, and she doubted if Howard's stiff-necked mother would settle for any other way of officially breaking up the marriage.

She noticed a yacht sidling into the bay and wondered idly whose it was. Sir Victor Quarley had one. She wondered if Tania were still a guest in his party or whether Tania and Felicity had returned to London. Anything, Ann thought, anything to think about, so that her mind didn't stray back to the utter sweetness of lying in Howard's arms last night. That was a closed book, his manner had said this morning.

But he had promised, she reminded herself angrily, not to require anything of her that she didn't want to give! Then she recalled how she had fallen against him, when he had been going to kiss her. There was invitation! And could she blame him if he chose to think that she had been encouraging Tom Westbury after all she had said about not wanting anything but an arranged marriage?

The shops were quiet at that time in the morning. Ann bought a new Sunday dress for Opal, for the warmer weather they might expect, and some more jerseys and cardigans. Chiefly, however, she wanted to replace the dress she was wearing. Replace it so that she need never remember it again. She would give it away – no, nobody else must wear it. She would destroy it, somehow. Perhaps Jago would get it burned for her if she tied it up in a parcel.

Jago... Where had he been these last few days, since the row over his being out on the moor with her and the child? Why did they all make such a fuss about that young man? He was goodness itself, in his simple way. True, he had a wild violent temper when animals were being hurt, but was that such a bad thing? Too much cruelty existed towards small things.

Reluctantly, at last, after lunch out, Ann knew she must return to Kingsbride. Tensely she sat, clutching her parcels. The offending dress had been parcelled up for her, and she wore a quiet grey jersey suit with a hand-printed silk blouse of grey and muted blues, and a thread of silver through the design. On any other occasion she would have loved it, and the new grey court shoes, gloves and bag to match. Today she had no pleasure in anything. What she must do would take all the energy and resolve in her. She must settle the future for Opal, no matter what was likely to happen to Ann herself.

A man flagged down the car near the gates of Kingsbride. It was Tom Westbury. Burridge stopped for him. Tom spoke pleasantly to him and got a smiling answer which surprised Ann. Then he opened the back door of the car to speak to her.

'Ann, I wanted to see you to say goodbye. I'm going, but there was a bit of a flap on at the house. They didn't seem to know where you were!' he explained.

'That's nonsense. Isn't my ... my husband back? He walked – that is, he left the car for me to go into town shopping. Wasn't he there?'

'No, he caught an early train to London, but he'd told them you'd be back within the hour. That was early this morning, I gather.'

She looked in some confusion at the stiff back of Burridge, who was listening even though he was making an excellent pretence of being deaf.

'Get in the car and talk to me. No, better still, it's such a nice day. Let's walk, and Burridge can take the car and my shopping to the house for me.'

Either way it wasn't a very good plan, for Burridge would have to say that Ann had gone off with her man friend from London, or he would have had the pleasure of hearing every word they said, in the back of the car. Ann was annoyed and said so, when she and Tom had walked on, and the car turned off into the Kingsbride drive.

'Tom, did you have to do that? I'm in such trouble in the house already.'

Tom said stolidly, 'As I understand it, from Mrs Thornton, you are being very badly treated over this queer job of yours. Why you undertook it, I can't think. Didn't you know it was a put-up job for him to get the inheritance and then the lawyers would dissolve the marriage later on?'

With the memory of the night before still so fresh, the high colour burned in her cheeks, but she said coolly enough, 'Dear Tom, don't you know enough about Mrs Thornton yet to know she's my enemy and that she's doing her best to have this marriage broken up?'

'No, love, no, you've got it all wrong! Oh, I know a lot of people don't like her, but she's really a very kind person. She's told me a lot about this Howard Crayne and his mother, and how they exploit everyone when it suits them.'

'Well!' Ann exploded. 'That's a good one, from her! She wanted to marry Howard, and she and his mother are such great friends, I don't know what's going on!'

Tom continued to smile and shake his

head. 'You're so gullible, Ann! How people do manage to make you believe what they want to!'

'Yes, don't they just!' she said heatedly. 'Look, I am staying here, for good, as Howard's wife–'

'But that's just what you're not going to do, love. I'm telling you – he's gone up to London only this morning to see the solicitors–'

'Yes, I know about that. But that isn't about our marriage but about something that's come up about Opal. I can't tell you, Tom, because it's private and personal.'

Tom looked at her with such sadness that she felt like shaking him. 'Don't look like that, Tom! Believe me, Minerva's been playing her own game right up to our marriage, which she tried to put off as you well know, by giving Felicity something to give to me to make me ill and postpone the wedding – and it did, if you remember!'

'But it's not true, Ann. Felicity wouldn't–'

'She didn't know what it was. Minerva told her it would do me good,' Ann said, desperately, but it was no use. She just couldn't convince Tom. 'Oh, my goodness, that Minerva's really got you round her little finger, hasn't she? Well, there's nothing else I can say, my dear, but to thank you for feeling you had to advise me. But believe me, it's all right. I can manage.'

'What will you do?' he asked curiously.

'Do? What his mother suggested I should do a day or two ago – learn how to be a good chatelaine of Kingsbride and to be a good wife to Howard. Well, at least it will please his mother and take the pressure off there.'

Tom pursed his lips. 'I'll stick around for another week. I'm not satisfied that everything will go as you want it to. You're so stubborn, you won't listen to me. They're using you, love, and Mrs Thornton has been good enough to warn me, and I won't have it said that she's anything else but a good kind woman!'

Ann left him at last and walked slowly back to Kingsbride. Mrs Farraker was not in sight but Minerva sailed out of the Green Salon. She hadn't been persuaded by Howard to go to London with him, then!

Minerva pulled up short with a start, at the sight of Ann. 'What are *you* doing here? Why aren't you with that child?'

'With Opal? How could I be? I've only just returned. Burridge brought me back–' Ann broke off, biting her lip in confusion. Burridge hadn't brought her back. He had dropped her at the gates to go for a walk with Tom Westbury.

Minerva said, 'Burridge came back alone, presumably having dropped Howard at the station. If you haven't seen Opal, who *did* she go off with, then?'

Ann's knees gave way and she sat down. 'Go off with? Look, tell me this slowly, from the beginning. Where am I supposed to have taken Opal?'

'I can't stop talking with you!' Minerva exploded. 'Something must be done about it! Goodness, you must know very well that Opal's been worrying to go on Sir Victor's yacht and now suddenly he said she could, if she was accompanied by an adult. The last I saw of the child was dashing out calling to someone that she was ready and I heard a car start up, but by the time I got to the window it had turned the corner of the drive and–'

'How long ago was this?' Ann demanded. 'And where was she supposed to be going?'

'As if you didn't know! To the harbour, of course! I advise you to get moving – if that child gets to the harbour, they'll pick her up and she'll be on that yacht without you and what will Howard say about that when he hears?'

'But who was she with? Good heavens, why did this have to happen?'

'It might not have, if you'd done what you told Howard you would do – come here at once,' Minerva said. 'What happened to you?'

'Don't tell me there's something you don't know!' Ann flashed angrily. It wasn't often she retorted, but this was infuriating. In his present mood, Howard would be too angry to listen to anything, and he would have no patience with poor little Opal. He had shown that yesterday.

Minerva shrugged and departed. Quite clearly she was going to be no help at all. Ann didn't expect it. Ann rushed down to the garages, but Burridge and the big car were nowhere to be seen. Perhaps Burridge had taken Opal, expecting to pick Ann up as she returned from her walk with Tom Westbury?

She hurried down the drive on foot, hoping to catch him, but there was no sign of him or the child. Only the doctor, driving slowly by. He pulled up and offered Ann a lift, which she gladly accepted, but he was elderly and preoccupied, and Ann didn't like to burden him with this wild tale of Minerva's. Better to get to the harbour and see if the child was there. Probably disconsolately waiting on a bollard, for Ann to arrive.

The doctor insisted on going right to the entrance of the harbour. 'Going for a sail?' he asked kindly. 'I wouldn't go too far. Never did trust a sky like this in this county! That'll be a storm for sure! Put it off till Howard takes you.'

'No, I'm not going for a sail. I have to meet someone,' Ann said quickly, and as he raised his eyebrows at that, she said, 'I have to see someone going on Sir Victor's yacht.'

The doctor pursed his lips. He had heard some odd things about this marriage. He would have said that Howard's choice of a wife was unsuitable. She was a nice little thing, but no match for old Mrs Crayne's scheming. Now here the girl was, all confused about a yacht party run by Sir Victor. It didn't look good.

'What does your husband think about letting you out with a sky like that?' he ventured, but Ann was already stumbling out of the car. 'Got to rush,' she said. 'Thanks for the lift!' and she hurtled down the slope to where stores were being put aboard the small craft waiting to go out to the big yacht.

'I'm not too late!' she thought, and rushed up to one of the seamen. 'Has a little girl gone out to the yacht? A little dark girl with glasses?' but they were all of mixed nationality and had no English except the last man to come staggering out of a shop with more stores. They referred Ann to him, but she might have saved herself the trouble. 'Not to worry, ducks,' he said, handing her aboard and not listening. 'I've been told to look out for you. Everything's in order.'

Ann thought dazedly, how comforting it was to hear English spoken. She got in and they rapidly left the harbour behind. It was then that she noticed the other seamen were looking oddly at her. At first she thought it was because her suit wasn't right for a party on a yacht. Then she began to get rather disturbed about the way they spoke in low tones in their own language, leering a little in her direction. Her uneasiness increased, but the Cornish sky was an impossible pearly shade, without a single cloud. How could the doctor's warning about the weather be regarded? He had no idea, she told herself. And then she remembered it had been like this yesterday...

Howard had never been in such a bad temper, his mother thought. She had tried tears and one of her famous fainting fits, and had run Gertrude off her feet, but what with Howard's rage and the storm outside, Mrs Crayne really did begin to feel ill.

'Howard, I do not know about any of these things, and I do not know what happened to Minerva. If she isn't in the house, then I believe you, she has gone out, and I hope she will be held up somewhere because of the storm, for being so inconsiderate. But I do not know what happened to your wife, and I do not know where the child is. You must ask the staff.'

Minerva came out of her room as he left his mother's suite. 'Oh, Howard, you're back! I've been so unwell, and so worried. Ever since Ann went—'

'Good heavens, at last I can get some sense out of someone. Yes, where did Ann go, and when?'

'If you're going to shout at me, I shall go back into my room,' she said.

'Minerva, I warn you, I am not in a mood to be trifled with, tonight. I have had a very nasty day and I want Ann. I want her at once. There are things I have to say to her. Where did she go?'

'I only know what Burridge and the doctor said,' Minerva told him, with a hand to her head as a fresh clap of thunder seemed to split the roof of Kingsbride.

'What did they say?' Howard asked, between his teeth.

She shrugged. 'Burridge said she'd asked to be dropped off to walk with that Tom Westbury, who had been waiting for her at the gates.'

Howard said, 'Go on,' and Minerva was glad she wasn't Ann.

'The doctor said he later gave her a lift down to the harbour to go on board Sir Victor's yacht. It's a party,' she finished unnecessarily.

Howard looked as if he were going to explode. 'And where is Opal?'

'Howard, honestly, does anyone know what that child gets up to. *I* don't know!'

She left Howard ringing the doctor's house, to have Minerva's story confirmed.

The doctor added that he had warned Ann that the weather looked bad but she hadn't listened. No, she hadn't said who she was going on board the yacht with.

'Are you sure it wasn't the child?' Howard pressed. Anything to squash a story that his mother would soon turn against him. Any young woman locally who went aboard the Quarley yacht was regarded with raised eyebrows. Not his Ann, he thought. Westbury might have been with her, but he couldn't persuade the doctor to admit that there had been a man waiting for her. She had gone out with the crew and their stores. Gone alone.

He went back to his mother. 'I am going to send a radio message to Quarley about that yacht of his,' Howard said. 'But while I am doing that, I require you, Mother, without argument, to make Minerva understand that I want her out of this house. And don't say she's your guest, because I want you to go too. Don't look at me like that. There is the cottage. That, or I will find you a flat, but meantime you go to an hotel. No, not perhaps in this storm, but as soon as it is over. And no arguments.'

'You're inhuman!' his mother gasped. 'Gertrude, tell my son he's gone raving mad. Tell him my health won't stand a move – I cannot stay in an hotel!'

Gertrude looked at Howard, and he

paused, a lot of his anger seeping away. She had the oddest look on her face. Happiness would have been too strong a word but certainly satisfaction was there. 'I think I would go to an hotel if I were you, madam, a nice hotel, that is. You see, you can't stay here without me to look after you, now can you? You must have good service.'

'Where will you be? I haven't given you leave to go anywhere!'

'I have tried to tell you twice today, ma'am, but you were ... preoccupied. I am going to marry Burridge, and of course I'll have all my work cut out to look after him, won't I?'

Howard would have liked to stay and hear what went on next, but he needed to radio the yacht, and besides, he didn't want to be involved with his mother and Gertrude. Fancy old Gertrude, keeping quiet about her romance all this time! Fancy Burridge, not saying anything!

The phone lines were so bad with the storm, that he had to give up after a while. Finally he contacted the police to help him and went in search of Opal.

She came out of the attic door, dirty, dishevelled, tear-streaked. 'Where the devil have you been?' he demanded. 'Look at the state you're in! And what happened to Ann? Did you see her when she came back this morning?'

'I don't know where she is,' Opal sobbed. 'She didn't come home last night, and that Minerva told me she was with Mr Westbury, in his rooms in the pub in the village. But Ann wouldn't do that, would she? She wouldn't, she wouldn't!'

Howard was shocked. 'No, she wouldn't,' he said firmly. 'Ann and I stayed at a farm. We got caught in the rain and she was likely to get another chill. They put her to bed, with a fire in the bedroom.' And all the while he said reasonable things to the child, his mind kept shouting, 'It's true, what Ann always said – Minerva spread lies about her!

'Minerva is going,' he told Opal, in a voice she had to believe. 'And when Ann comes back, we three are going to live cosily in Kingsbride together. My mother is going to live in an hotel and Gertrude is to marry Burridge and make him comfortable. Now, won't that all be nice?' But all the time his mind kept up a tattoo: Ann won't come back, never, never!

Opal almost echoed it. 'Bad things are happening tonight. Ann won't come back. That Minerva sent her away. I heard her.'

It was some time before Howard could get a coherent account from Opal, who had been well hidden at the time. Finally he discovered that she had found the way into an old shaft, and fallen on the secret of Kingsbride. A ventilation system that had been built in by a former Crayne in the times of the Troubles where he could lie hidden listening in to his guests in the state rooms and his guests' servants in their quarters below stairs. His way of nipping treachery in the bud. Whether Opal realised what she had discovered, was doubtful, but she could tell him clearly how it applied to herself. 'I told you there were voices in the air,' she said.

She seemed to expect Howard to contradict this but when he didn't she offered: 'I knew there had to be some good reason, because the doors are too thick to hear through and there aren't any keyholes.'

He nodded encouragingly, so she continued, 'I found a book which says it works by pumping air, and the sounds go with it. I don't understand this but I believe it. The sounds come out through little holes in the pattern of the carving on the walls. On the other side you can see a light showing through. I'll show you.'

He wanted to see for himself, badly, but there was no more opportunity. The police, who had been trying to send his radio message to the yacht, had to tell him that it had foundered on the rocks off the headland, not far down the coast.

Opal crept away to her room and sat shivering. Gertrude found her there soon afterwards. 'Don't worry, my lamb. Mr

Howard has gone to the cove to see if he can ... find Ann for us. There will be a lot of people there, putting out lines to the yacht to rescue people. Don't worry.'

Opal said, 'He won't find her. He would if he took Jago. Jago will know how to find her. They say Jago's peculiar, not-all-there, but he loves Ann and he'll know how to find her. Why don't you tell that to Uncle Howard? He won't listen to me, but he'd listen to you! Tell him!'

Gertrude said gently, 'Your Uncle Howard might listen to me but Jago's mother wouldn't let him go.'

They were startled by a voice at the door. 'Yes, she would!' Mrs Farraker said. How long she had been standing there, they didn't know. 'I'll send my son. Then the master will see what a good useful boy he is, and not mind him staying on here.'

Jago couldn't go fast enough, but to Howard, the next few hours had a nightmare quality that he didn't care to remember afterwards. The Quarley yacht was the last word in luxury but it didn't mean that the modern equipment could keep it from sure disaster on the old jagged teeth of the rocks beyond Toley Head. Howard supposed that men and women had stood helpless on this stretch of beach over the centuries, and would again in the future; helplessly wondering what was the use of modern equipment and aid when the sea was just the same and the storm winds as terrible as they had ever been. He stood there going over all that had passed in the little while that he had known Ann, and he was quite sure he would never see her again.

Jago's bulk was vaguely comforting beside him. Occasionally the handsome giant made an angry sound in his throat, but most of the time he stood there helpless, waiting for Howard to tell him what to do. But Howard couldn't tell him. One lifeboat had already overturned. The lines they had hurled to the foundering ship had not been able to make their mark. Howard stood racking his brains, wondering if there had been anything overlooked that anyone could do. And then he recalled what Ann had said when he had been so angry that day, the day her engagement ring had been lost in the water. Ann and the child might think Howard hadn't been aware of its loss, but he had guessed. Only the fact that his awakening love for her, had stopped him from making the fuss that she had expected. Now he remembered that Ann had said Jago was fantastically strong and a superb swimmer and diver.

He himself was no mean performer in the water, but Ann didn't know that. Now he said, his ear close to Jago's, 'I could swim out there with a line but I'd need help. Can you hear me?'

Jago nodded, and repeated. 'Help, yes. Find Ann.'

Howard frowned. The fellow was not really all there. But Ann's voice insisted in his mind that if you spoke slowly, a few words at a time, Jago understood. He tried again. 'To save Ann – swim out with line – a *line* – could you help save Ann?' And this time not only Jago understood but others heard and in no time the pair of them were being equipped, Jago bursting with eagerness to go.

And then the nightmare began.

When it was all over and he was sitting by Ann's side in a small room in the hospital in Venfold, he thought with a shudder of the mighty breakers, their terrible power, and the unimaginable cold of the sea. He lived with the half-formed fear of what his housekeeper would have to say if he didn't see that her son was returned safely, but it was Jago in the end who saved both Ann and himself. Jago had the brute strength and the doglike devotion for Ann.

But that was hours and hours ago...

Suddenly, Ann's voice, soft yet clear, cut through his tired mind. 'Howard? You here?' But he couldn't speak, and she slipped away again.

But later, when she next opened her eyes, she had plenty to say. 'Tell me all about it again,' she begged, so he went over it again. 'Tell me Opal's safe,' and he reassured her of that.

He couldn't think how long he had been sitting by her bed, holding her hand as if scared to let it go, and flinching from the memory of Jago's face because they wouldn't let him go into her room and see she was alive; flinching from how he would face Opal if Ann finally didn't recover from this. Hours of turmoil with his own thoughts; hours of snatched too-heavy sleep until he was allowed to be with Ann again. And then at last they were all sure she would be all right.

Mrs Farraker had sent a pot of growing flowers for Ann's bedside. Jago had made a fuss because they wouldn't take Ann his gift of a new kitten. Opal sent a heartbreaking smudged letter, which was almost all crosses to denote kisses, and the passionate plea, 'Don't die, don't die, Ann, don't die!' and even his mother had sent a severe, but correctly couched note wishing Ann back to good health.

But sooner or later Ann knew she would have to explain why she was on the yacht. 'Minerva sent me,' she said simply. 'I had to go, to be with Opal, only she wasn't on the quay, and the crew were smiling in a peculiar way. It was that sort of party, though I didn't realise it at first. How come

Lady Quarley is so nice, if Sir Victor is like that?'

'My dear love, my dear little love,' Howard choked, 'how can I be sure you won't go off on another wild goose chase like this?'

'I won't, if you stay with me,' Ann murmured.

He couldn't believe she had said that. 'Do you mean it, Ann?'

She hesitated. 'That night, at the farm ... did you mean ... all *that*?' she whispered, and when he said angrily, 'Of course! What made you think I might not?' she said, 'It was your face, next morning. So cold, so remote. And you went and left me, as if it was just ... one of those things. I assumed you were sorry you'd ... not kept your promise to yourself, about it only being a business arrangement.'

'Dear love, you weren't looking too happy yourself, and I was angry that we had to do it in such a fashion, so secretly, because of Minerva and my mother being there. But they're not there any more. I sent Minerva away, and I told my mother to go and live in an hotel.'

Ann stared, then her mouth turned down. 'No, I can't believe that. Don't joke, Howard. It's too serious.'

'I am not joking! My mother went. Not merely on my account – Gertrude told her she would have nobody to look after her.

Gertrude disclosed that she was to marry Burridge so my mother would have nobody to look after her any more.'

'Oh-h!' Ecstasy filled Ann's face. 'So Kingsbride is ours!'

'If you want it to be. Do you, dear one?'

'Oh, yes, yes with you and Opal and Mrs Farraker and everyone.'

'And Burridge and Gertrude, who are sure we can't get on without them.'

'Oh, yes, with those two as well. *And* the animals?'

'*And* the animals,' he sighed in mock resignation. '*And* Jago.'

The following day Ann was almost ready to be allowed to leave hospital and wanted to know all about Opal, where she had been while Ann was being sent to the yacht, and why had she been sent without Opal?

Howard considered her. 'To discredit you in my eyes, as you would have been if you'd gone alone to that sort of party. Minerva, no mean psychologist, had worked that out. But Opal told me the truth. She had been listening to Minerva's skill in persuading you to go on your own.'

He told a deeply interested Ann about the secret of the shaft the child had found. 'We must have builders in, to do something about that, or nothing will ever be private and personal again,' he frowned, but after some thought, Ann objected.

'No, it will mean destroying the place. Let's leave it as it is, for the public to see. Let's make over the rooms Opal and I had, for our personal use. They are safe from eavesdroppers.' He loved Kingsbride so much, that he agreed.

After a while, he stopped kissing her to let her frame another question. 'Opal – did she ever get back the rest of her letter?'

'Oh, yes, that letter. Minerva had it. I made her give it to me, though she insisted, of course, that she'd found it in the corridor and couldn't even read the writing.' He smiled. 'There was nothing else worth reading in it – it was just Elaine trying to be kind to a child who wasn't her own. Trying to make up for it all.'

'But Opal isn't a relative and there won't be anything from the old uncle's will, do you think?' Ann murmured, all her thoughts devotedly leaping ahead to Opal's future protection.

'Indeed there will. It's rather odd. The old uncle had apparently guessed Opal wasn't Elaine's child. Don't ask me how, but he'd left a letter (which he didn't want read out at the time of his Will being read) in which he said he liked Opal for herself, though he didn't love her enough to have her brought up in his house. He preferred to leave her with a succession of foster mothers. Well, I can't pretend to understand that. He was old and ill and eccentric, but he did say in his letter, that he'd been to see Opal once, without letting her know who he was, and what went on between them must have impressed him. He refers to her as a "gallant little wretch", and that she was to inherit just the same as if she'd been Elaine's own child. She's quite rich.'

Ann smiled. 'Yes, I know, and I don't mean her diamond necklace which I hope she showed to you.'

Opal had forgotten to show Howard, it seemed, and he had been too distracted to ask to see the box with the false bottom. He looked quite startled.

'Don't worry, it will be safe with her. It's her treasure,' Ann said. 'And she's mine.'

Howard sat playing with her hands, putting them abstractedly to his lips now and again. He had little fund of loverlike words, but his hands, she had discovered, could be very tender. 'Is she your only treasure?' he murmured.

'No!' She was shocked. 'I have many. All my friends – Gertrude, Mrs Farraker, even old Burridge. Oh, and animals, and especially Jago.'

'No other treasure?'

'Oh, I almost forgot,' she teased. 'My husband. My careless, hectoring, handsome husband, who got me casually through a newspaper advertisement, and forgot to give me a honeymoon until we got soaked in the rain.'

She couldn't breathe for a little while, he smothered her with so many kisses. But when he had almost embraced her to sleepiness, and she almost didn't hear what he was saying, he murmured, 'You forgot to mention Kingsbride,' and when she agreed, he whispered, for her ears alone, 'And the heirs to love it and maintain it, after we're gone.'

She agreed, rather breathlessly. At times he was too masculine for words. But he hadn't finished. 'I know it wasn't a requirement of the job, but what do you think of your hectoring, casual, overbearing husband?'

'He's a tyrant,' she said, 'but I love him, with all my heart.'

The publishers hope that this book has given you enjoyable reading. Large Print Books are especially designed to be as easy to see and hold as possible. If you wish a complete list of our books please ask at your local library or write directly to:

Dales Large Print Books
Magna House, Long Preston,
Skipton, North Yorkshire.
BD23 4ND

This Large Print Book, for people
who cannot read normal print,
is published under the auspices of

THE ULVERSCROFT FOUNDATION

... we hope you have enjoyed this book.
Please think for a moment about those
who have worse eyesight than you ...
and are unable to even read or enjoy
Large Print without great difficulty.

You can help them by sending a
donation, large or small, to:

**The Ulverscroft Foundation,
1, The Green, Bradgate Road,
Anstey, Leicestershire, LE7 7FU,
England.**
or request a copy of our brochure for
more details.

The Foundation will use all donations
to assist those people who are visually
impaired and need special attention
with medical research, diagnosis
and treatment.

Thank you very much for your help.